It's not as if he wanted to date Libby.

Carson stilled, the thought surprising him. Where had that come from? The last thing he had time for right now was a girlfriend. Most of his time and energy needed to be devoted to his business.

"You must know how anxious I am to start my shift, Mr. Davies," Libby said.

If she'd said the words with more enthusiasm, Carson would have believed them. But he had the feeling that his newest employee would much prefer basking in the sun to waiting on the lunch crowd.

"I'll have Erin orient you."

Libby scooted back her chair and stood, holding out her hand. "It's been a pleasure, Mr. Davies."

"Carson," he said, his hand taking hers and lingering a moment longer than necessary. "We don't stand on ceremony here."

And with that, Libby moved across the floor with the casual grace of a dancer, her head held high.

There was something intriguing about her. And something that said there was more to this new waitress than met the ey

Books by Cynthia Rutledge

Love Inspired

Unforgettable Faith #102
Undercover Angel #123
The Marrying Kind #135
Redeeming Claire #151
Judging Sara #157
Wedding Bell Blues #178
A Love To Keep #208
The Harvest #223
   "Loving Grace"
Two Hearts #246

CYNTHIA RUTLEDGE

loves writing romance because a happy ending is guaranteed! Writing for Steeple Hill allows her to combine her faith in God with her love of romance. When she's not working full-time as a regional consultant for a large insurance company or writing romance, Cynthia likes to chat with her daughter, Wendy, for long hours on the phone, take walks with her husband, Kirt, and cat (Oreo) and have lunch with her friends.

Two Hearts is Cynthia's ninth book for Steeple Hill Love Inspired. Cynthia loves to hear from readers and encourages you to visit her Web site at www.cynthiarutledge.com.

TWO HEARTS

CYNTHIA RUTLEDGE

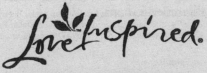

Published by Steeple Hill Books™

STEEPLE HILL BOOKS

Steeple
Hill®

ISBN 0-373-87256-9

TWO HEARTS

Visit us at www.steeplehill.com

Printed in U.S.A.

You may say to yourself, My power and the strength of my hands have produced this wealth for me. But remember the LORD your God, for it is He who gives you the ability to produce wealth, and so confirms His covenant, which He swore to your forefathers, as it is today.

—*Deuteronomy* 8:17-18

To my good friend, Susan Powers Alexander.
You're the best!

Chapter One

"So aren't you the least bit tempted to call him?" Sierra Summers stuck her spoon into the hot fudge sundae and took a big bite. "Get his side of the story?"

"Are you crazy?" Libby Carlyle couldn't believe her longtime friend would even ask such a question. The moment Libby had seen her boyfriend leaving that crowded theater with his arm around another woman, it had been over. In the past couple of weeks she'd suspected his interest might be waning. Now, she wished she'd gotten rid of him right off instead of giving him the benefit of the doubt. "Stephen is history. All I can say is good riddance."

Sierra's gaze narrowed. She opened her mouth then closed it.

Libby shifted uncomfortably under the penetrating

stare. Sierra knew how much she'd liked Stephen and the hopes she'd once held for their relationship. But she also knew how hard it was for Libby to admit she cared.

After what seemed an eternity, Sierra shrugged, licked the fudge from her spoon and returned her attention to her sundae.

Libby breathed a sigh of relief and settled back in the rustic chair. She glanced around the quaint interior of the restored warehouse, suddenly glad they'd decided to stop at The Chocolate Factory on the way home. Though seeing Stephen had put a damper on the evening, a healthy dose of ice cream was a guaranteed pick-me-up. Libby smiled. "This is like old times. Like when we were teenagers."

Life had been so carefree then. Even though Sierra had gone to a public high school and Libby had been sent to a private boarding school back east, they'd spent their summers hanging out in places like this—eating ice cream, drinking Coke and talking about boys.

Life had been so simple. All she'd had to worry about was wearing stylish clothes and having a date for Saturday night. But by the time she'd reached her mid-twenties, a Saturday-night date was no longer enough.

Life had become more complex. You didn't just date, you fell in love. Then you became engaged, got married and had babies. It was a natural evolution.

Unfortunately Libby could never seem to get past the dating game. Love came easily to other women, but not to her. Men always liked her at first but after a few weeks or a few months they got restless and moved on.

For a long time, Libby hadn't given it much thought. After all, didn't they say you had to kiss a lot of frogs before you found your prince? But she'd done her share of kissing and had yet to get out of the frog pond.

It had made her worry that maybe she had some kind of fatal flaw, something in her personality that made her unlovable. She felt she had to at least consider the possibility. After all, her own parents didn't love her. Her father had left when she was ten and never looked back. And she and her mother had never been close. Libby heaved a heartfelt sigh.

"It will all work out for the best." Sierra reached across the table and gave Libby's hand a reassuring pat.

"Did I tell you he said he loved me?" Libby shook her head. "Of course I knew better. He was just saying it, hoping I'd give in and do something I know I'd regret."

"Stephen wasn't the right one for you," Sierra said softly. Pushing her sundae to the side, she leaned forward and rested her arms on the table. "Pastor always says that when things go bad in our life, God finds a way to give a blessing. Mark my words, something good is going to come of all this.''

Though Libby believed in God, she wasn't feeling too blessed at the moment. And, regardless of what Sierra thought, Libby knew that the only good that would come of this whole thing was that she'd be more on her guard the next time. ''I can't believe he fooled me.''

''It could have been worse. You could have married the guy and then found out what he was like.'' A shadow crossed Sierra's face and Libby knew she was thinking of her failed marriage to Jerry the Jerk.

''I *am* grateful it didn't get that far,'' Libby said. ''*Very* grateful.''

She'd rather spend the rest of her life alone, than end up with the wrong man. But it was so easy to be fooled. What if her trip to San Francisco hadn't been canceled? What if she'd turned down Sierra's invitation to the movie? Would she have ever known Stephen was cheating on her?

Libby shoved the questions aside but the uneasiness remained. She'd always trusted her instincts, depended on them to keep her out of bad situations. But she'd wanted to believe in Stephen so much that she'd ignored the red flags.

If she wasn't careful, she'd end up a three-time loser like her mother. Stella Carlyle was a sucker for a handsome man with a smooth line. After her third divorce Stella had waxed philosophical, saying at least there had always been love in her marriages. Of course, it had been her money that the men were in love with, not her.

"Sometimes I think it would have been easier if I'd been born poor," Libby said with a sudden burst of insight. "Maybe it isn't my personality that's the problem, maybe it's the money. Maybe it attracts the wrong kind of men."

Sierra tilted her head then broke out into laughter. "Now I've heard everything."

"I'm serious." Libby searched her mind for something to support her theory. "It says in the Bible, money is the root of all evil."

"I think it's *the love of* money that's the root of all evil." Sierra rolled her eyes and chuckled. "Anyway, since when do you read the Bible?"

Libby ignored the question. Although she'd spent more than her fair share of time in church, Libby had secretly thought that God had always reserved His loving kindness for other, more deserving girls. Still, she had to admit that right now those Bible verses she'd learned as a child were coming in handy.

"It is written money can't buy happiness." It might not be a true Bible quote, but Libby figured it was close enough. And it certainly fit her current situation.

"Trust me, money may not buy happiness, but it can sure help," Sierra said. "If you don't believe me, ask any poor person."

Libby could tell by Sierra's tone that her friend had no idea that money could be anything but a tremendous blessing. But then, how could she? She'd never had people be nice to her just because of her family connections. She'd never had a man say he loved her, when all he loved was her money. She'd never known how poor you could feel, even with millions in the bank.

As she and Sierra talked, a crazy idea that had been lingering in the back of Libby's mind took hold.

It was outrageous.

It made no sense.

But it was so intriguing.

"Sierra." Libby leaned forward and rested her arms on the terra-cotta table, excitement coursing up her spine. "I've got a proposition for you...."

Chapter Two

Maybe this wasn't such a good idea after all.

Libby stood for a moment outside the weathered wood building, rethinking her part of the impetuous bargain. But the switch had been her idea and if she didn't go in soon, she would be late for work—or rather, Sierra would be late. And her friend needed this job in order to pay her fall tuition.

Squaring her shoulders, Libby grabbed the over-size door handle, pulled it open and stepped inside. She entered the airy foyer and let the door close behind her.

She widened her gaze. The place was more impressive than what she'd imagined. It was large and open with two main areas for wining and dining, including a glass-topped atrium. Sierra had also raved about an open-air garden deck where patrons could sip their favorite drink and gaze out over the water while enjoying the ocean breeze.

The trendy restaurant and bar had been in business for about a year. During that time, Carson's Waterfront had quickly become known as *the* place in Santa Barbara to enjoy a designer drink, watch widescreen sports and listen to live music. But until this moment Libby had never been inside to appreciate the extensive remodeling.

"May I help you?" A perky redhead who looked as if she should be leading cheers at the local high school, flashed a friendly smile.

"I'm Sierra Summers," Libby said. "I'm here to see Mr. Davies."

"Why don't you have a seat?" The girl waved Libby to a chair at a nearby table. "I'll let Carson know you're here."

Libby returned the girl's smile and took a seat in a slatted wood chair with curved chrome arms, glad she didn't have to worry about Carson Davies taking one look and realizing she wasn't Sierra Summers.

According to Sierra, the man who'd hired her had quit and she hadn't met any of the other workers when she'd interviewed. That made taking Sierra's place a piece of cake.

Though Sierra had worked since she was sixteen in many different types of jobs, Libby's own work experience was more limited. During college she'd interned with a Wall Street firm and after graduation she'd bought her own antique store. She'd never waited tables before but she had eaten out a lot. It didn't look too tough.

"Ms. Summers?"

The deep masculine voice pulled Libby from her reverie. Her head jerked up.

"You must be Mr. Davies." Libby rose to her feet and extended her hand, pleased she could sound so calm while her insides were flip-flopping.

Dressed in a pair of khakis and a polo shirt, the man before her couldn't be more than thirty. With a lean muscular body, sun-bleached blond hair and brilliant blue eyes he looked as though he belonged on the beach playing volleyball, rather than in a restaurant, orienting a new waitress.

"Call me Carson," he said, giving her hand a perfunctory shake and flashing a smile that showed a mouthful of perfect white teeth.

"And you can call me…Libby." It was a calculated move, but one she had to take. There was no way she could spend the entire summer answering to "Sierra."

"Libby?" His gaze lowered to the clipboard in his hands. A frown marred his handsome brow. "I thought your name was Sierra?"

"It is," she hastened to reassure him. "But as you can see my middle initial is L, which stands for Lisabeth. I go by Libby."

Though she'd been able to say the whole sentence

without taking a breath, Libby was winded by the time she got to the end and more than a little apprehensive. She could only pray he'd buy the goofy explanation for the name change. Thankfully, Sierra's middle name—Lynn—*did* start with an *L,* so on the surface her reasoning made sense.

"Libby." He rolled the name around on his tongue as if testing the sound, then smiled. "Libby, it is."

Libby breathed a sigh of relief. So far, so good.

"Did Jack show you around?"

"Jack?"

"The guy who hired you?" he prompted.

"The short bald-headed one," she blurted, remembering the simple description Sierra had given her.

Carson laughed and a dimple flashed in his left cheek. "That's the one."

"I don't remember a tour," she said. "But it's been a while."

Carson tilted his head. "You were just hired last week."

Libby waved a dismissive hand. "Seven days is a long time."

"When you're without a waitstaff manager," Carson said, "it seems like forever."

"It's probably hard," Libby said, "losing such an important member of your team."

Sierra had told her the guy who'd hired her had emphasized that the boss was really into "teamwork'' so Libby decided it wouldn't hurt to toss that term around a bit.

"It was," Carson said. "But everyone has pulled together."

"Like a team," Libby said.

"Exactly," Carson responded, flashing another smile.

"So, Carson, are you from around here?" Libby resumed sitting, hoping Carson liked to talk about himself. She wasn't in any hurry to start waiting tables. If she was lucky, and he had a lot to say, she might be able to keep the conversation rolling long enough to get out of the lunch shift altogether.

"Let's just say I'm from the area." He took a seat in the chair opposite her. "I grew up in a small town about twenty miles north. And, other than the six years I spent in college back east, I've been right here."

Though she'd gone to Princeton, Libby had friends at most of the Ivy League schools. She wished she could ask him where he'd gone but she knew she couldn't pursue that topic without him figuring out she wasn't Sierra.

"How about you?" he asked in a conversational tone, smiling his thanks when the girl Libby had met earlier brought them each a glass of iced tea.

"I've lived here all my life," Libby said. "My mother is a housekeeper for a family in town and we live in a cottage on the grounds."

"What about your father?" he asked.

"He died when I was young." Libby racked her memory trying to remember what Sierra had told her about her dad. It hadn't been much. "In a car accident."

"My father died when I was little, too," Carson said. "There were three of us boys. And my dad didn't have much insurance."

"That must have been hard." Libby couldn't imagine raising three boys alone. Most days she could barely take care of herself.

"It wasn't easy," he said, shaking his head. "Mom did the best she could and we all helped out, but money was tight."

"It sounds like my childhood," Libby said. Actually, it sounded like Sierra's, but for the next three months she'd be living her life, so she might as well claim the history. "Except my plans to go away to school didn't work out and I ended up staying here. I'll graduate from UCSB in December."

Sierra had always been very private about her personal life, so Libby didn't elaborate. There was no reason for Carson to know that Sierra had been married and divorced by the time she was twenty-three. Or that she had a daughter. After all, Sierra might have agreed to trade places for the summer, but Maddie hadn't been part of the deal. The fact that Sierra was so protective of the little girl was understandable in light of all that had happened.

"Good for you," he said. "Any idea what you want to do when you finish?"

"I'm considering a few options," Libby hedged. "Did you always know you wanted to do this?" She swept her hand, indicating the large room.

Carson surveyed the restaurant and an unmistakable pride filled his gaze.

"I'd always dreamed of owning my own business," he said, and his eyes took on a faraway look. "I worked for a lot of people while growing up and I learned quite a bit. But what I really learned was that I wanted to be the one in charge, the one making the decisions, the one making the money."

Libby nodded even as a chill traveled up her spine at the determination in his voice. Her father had been handsome and ambitious. How far would Carson Davies go to further his career? Libby shoved the thought aside as of no importance. After all, what did it matter?

He was her boss.

She was his employee.

And after September, she'd never see him again.

Carson stared at the beautiful woman sitting across from him and wondered how long it would take Brian to make his move. Libby couldn't have started at a worse time. His business partner had just broken up with his girlfriend and was on the prowl.

And the dark-haired beauty with big blue eyes sitting in front of him was just the type of woman Brian liked. The question was for how long? Brian was a love 'em and leave 'em kind of guy. Carson had seen it happen over and over through the years. His friend reveled in the thrill of the chase, but once he had them, he quickly grew bored and moved on.

Though Carson didn't like the idea of his partner dating the help, Brian had so little to do with the day-to-day running of the business that there was no conflict of interest. Not like there would be if Carson wanted to date her.

He stilled, the thought surprising him. Where had that come from? The last thing he had time for right now was a girlfriend. Most of his time and energy needed to be devoted to making the business a success. And what extra time he had belonged to his family.

Brian didn't have such time commitments. And until now, Carson had never begrudged his partner his freewheeling lifestyle. But Carson didn't want to see Libby hurt. She seemed like a nice woman who'd had to work for everything, just like him. She didn't deserve to be blindsided by Brian. He'd just have to make sure that didn't happen.

"Do you furnish uniforms?"

Carson blinked and tried to clear his mind. "What did you say?"

"I asked if you furnished uniforms," Libby said

with a slight smile. "Everyone I've seen so far seems to be wearing khaki pants or shorts and green polos."

"Maybe we just all like the same type of clothes." Carson kept his face expressionless. "Did you ever think of that?"

"I did," Libby said with a twinkle in her eye. "But I immediately discarded that notion."

Carson was ready to continue to play along until he realized he was flirting. "Actually we start you off with two shirts," he said, reminding himself to stick to business. This was his employee, not some woman in a bar who'd caught his eye. "You can wear your choice of khaki shorts or pants."

"I'm afraid I didn't bring either with me today," Libby said with an unapologetic smile. "I don't think Jack mentioned a dress code. Or if he did, I must have forgotten."

"No problem," Carson said, glancing at her white pants. "We should have a shirt for you in the back and we'll just have to pretend those are bleached-out khakis."

Impulsively he gave her a wink, pleased when she laughed.

"You're so kind," she said. "You must have known how anxious I am to get started."

Though she didn't crack a smile, maybe if she'd said the words with a little more enthusiasm, Carson would have believed them. But he had the feeling that Ms. Libby Summers would much prefer to be outside basking in the sun, rather than waiting on the lunch crowd that should start arriving any minute.

"Erin." Carson waved over the girl who'd brought the iced tea to their table moments before. "This is Libby Summers. She's one of our new servers. I'd like you to take her to the back, pick out a couple of shirts and then maybe have her shadow you today. Libby is an experienced waitress so if you want to let her take a few tables that would be fine."

"Sure," Erin said. "I'll be glad to orient her."

Libby scooted her chair back and stood, holding out her hand. "It's been a pleasure to meet you, Mr. Davies."

"Carson," he reminded her, his hand taking hers and lingering a moment longer than necessary. "We don't stand on ceremony here."

"That's because we don't have time," Erin said with an impudent grin. "We're too busy working to do anything else."

Carson laughed.

"But that's good," Erin said, casting a quick sideways glance at Carson. "We like it that way."

"We do?" Libby's gaze was doubtful.

"Sure." Erin nodded. "After all, we're here for the money. No customers, no tips."

"That's right," Libby echoed. "No customers, no tips."

Carson stood and watched the two women walk toward the back of the restaurant. Erin chattered nonstop just as he'd expected, her ponytail swinging back and forth, her red hair gleaming in the fluorescent glare.

Next to her, Libby moved across the floor with the casual grace of a dancer, her hips gently swaying, her head held high.

There was something about Libby Summers.

Something that intrigued him.

And something that said there was more to this new waitress than met the eye.

Chapter Three

Near the end of the shift, Libby's new white pants were splattered with clam sauce and her shoes—which were the height of style, but not the height of comfort—had rubbed a blister on her big toe. Her stomach growled and her head ached. She longed to take a seat by the window, sip an ice-cold lemonade and have someone wait on *her*.

But Erin had only laughed when Libby had mentioned a break, and ordered her to take a pizza out to a table of fraternity boys. Libby had no choice but to comply. Even she could see that orders were backing up and the servers were swamped. Not only were they working two short, they'd gotten blasted with a busload of tourists.

Libby grabbed the large hamburger-mushroom and

headed to the dining room, sidestepping another server on the way out the swinging kitchen door.

Though the lunch crowd had started to thin, the room was still more than three-quarters full. Libby moved cautiously through the maze of tables, trying to keep the pressure off the foot with the blister. She passed Erin, who stood waiting patiently for an older woman to decide on her order, and they exchanged a smile. For the first time that day, Libby felt like part of the ''team.''

Still, just taking the pizza out was stressful and Libby couldn't help but breathe a sigh of relief when her final destination came into view. Keeping her gaze firmly fixed on the boys, Libby barely noticed the group of tourists gathering up their bags and purses at a large table to her left.

Looking back, Libby could only conclude the older gentleman must have been so intent on getting back to the bus that he didn't bother to look behind him before shoving his chair back from the table.

The unexpected force slamming into her leg pushed Libby off balance. She lurched sideways, desperately trying to right herself while still maintaining her hold on the pizza. But the aisle was narrow and her feet tangled together. The pizza went flying and Libby fell backward, hitting her head on the shiny hardwood floor.

Her breath came out in a whoosh and she saw stars. Pain shot through her right arm.

Libby closed her eyes. First day on the job and she'd ended up on the floor.

Could it get any worse?

"You don't have to do this." Libby stifled a groan and sat back against the leather seats of Carson's red Jeep, an ice bag pressed against her arm. "I'm sure it'll be fine."

"I want a doctor to check it out." Though he kept his eyes firmly on the road, Carson's voice was resolute and Libby knew she wasn't going to change his mind.

She'd already argued with him back at the restaurant but he'd insisted on personally driving her to a nearby UrgiCenter for X rays.

"I'm sorry," Libby said again. "I never meant for this to happen."

"Oh, come on now." Carson slanted her a sideways glance. "You really expect me to believe that falling and sending that pizza soaring like a Frisbee across the dining room was an accident?"

Libby paused. Though she may have considered many ways of getting out of working, falling wasn't one of them. And if she *had* planned to do something so crazy, she would have done it at the beginning of the shift, not at the end.

She opened her mouth to tell him just that when she noticed the gleam in his blue eyes. "Are you teasing me?"

His lips twitched. "What if I am?"

"You're a mean man." Though Libby kept her face expressionless she couldn't keep the smile from her voice.

"Mean, huh?"

Libby nodded. "The meanest."

Carson chuckled. "I'll consider that a compliment."

"You don't want to be mean," Libby said. "You want to be nice."

Carson stopped at a light and shifted his gaze to Libby. "And why would I want to be nice?"

"Because if you were nice, I might agree to have lunch with you after we get my arm X-rayed." The words popped out of Libby's mouth before she had a chance to stop them.

Carson's expression stilled and Libby cursed her impulsivity. She barely knew the guy, yet here she was coming on to him? That bump on the head must have affected her more than she realized.

"I've got an even better idea," he said. "How about I take you back to the restaurant after we see the doctor and the chef can cook you up whatever you want?"

Libby hadn't been born yesterday. It was clearly a "Thanks, but no thanks" reply. She should feel relieved. He'd saved them both from making a terrible mistake. After all, she was his employee. For the next ten weeks they needed to work together, and mixing business with pleasure was never a good idea.

"Perfect," she said as if that had been her intent all along. "See, I knew you were a nice guy."

For a second he looked nonplussed and she wondered if he'd expected her to protest. But if he thought that, he was mistaken.

Libby Carlyle didn't chase after any man.

She never had.

And she wasn't about to start now.

Libby glanced around the waiting room, looking for Carson. Though he'd offered to come back with her when she saw the doctor, she wasn't sure what kind of exam would be done so she'd declined.

She finally spotted him across the room reading a magazine. Instead of waiting to catch his eye, she walked over and tapped him on the shoulder. "All done."

"What did they say?" Carson immediately stood and her heart warmed at the obvious concern in his eyes.

"No break," she said. "Not even really sprained, just badly bruised. And the cut on the back of my head didn't need any stitches. He said in a couple of days I should be as good as new."

"How are you feeling?" Carson asked.

"My head still aches a little." Libby flexed and

extended her arm, then winced. "My arm hurts, but not as much as it did at first."

"Did he give you anything for the pain?"

"He didn't seem too worried, just said I should take ibuprofen." Libby shrugged. "But then he seemed in a hurry."

"I'm surprised." Carson smiled and his dimple flashed in his left cheek. "If I was the doctor and you were the patient, I would have definitely taken my time."

Libby returned his smile, thankful the comment didn't require a response, because at the moment she didn't have a clue what she'd say. Was he deliberately playing games or was he just naturally flirtatious?

"First day on the job and she hurts herself," Carson said with a rueful smile and a shake of his head. "I'm just keeping my fingers crossed you'll come back and give us another try."

"I have to come back," Libby said. Though she could easily afford to write out a check for Sierra's fall tuition, part of the deal had been she had to *earn* the money. "I need the money. Is there any chance you might have something for me to do while my arm is healing?"

"Don't worry about that," Carson said. "I'll find something. You don't by any chance have any experience with spreadsheets?"

"I sure do." Libby smiled, relieved to be back on familiar turf.

"Why don't you take a couple of days off, then, if you feel okay on Tuesday, come in about eight and we can go through some data I need entered."

"Eight?" Libby paused. Was the sun even up at that hour?

"Unless you prefer to start earlier?"

Was he joking? She rarely rolled out of bed before nine.

"I'll be there at eight," she said quickly. "Or maybe a little after."

"Whenever you get there will be fine," he said. "Just have someone page me."

"It's a plan," Libby said. "Now, how about that lunch you promised me?"

"Tell me about the new girl on the block." Brian Reiter took a sip of his martini and lifted an inquiring brow.

"Who?" Carson knew exactly what—or rather, who—his business associate was asking about, but for some reason he didn't want to discuss Libby. Especially not with Brian.

When she'd asked him to take her to lunch, Carson had wanted nothing more than to take her up on her offer. But he'd had to say no. No matter how much he was attracted to her, getting involved with an employee made no sense. Plus he didn't have time for a relationship. Taking care of Seth and Becca and making his business a success had to be his priorities.

"The new waitress," Brian said. "Word is she has a body that looks good in anything, and probably even better in nothing."

A wicked gleam filled Brian's eyes and Carson had to laugh. "I take it you and Sandi are still on the outs?"

"She says I only want one thing." Brian raised one hand and placed it dramatically over his heart. "Can you believe it?"

Carson laughed again. "Actually I can."

"Okay, so back to this new one," Brian said. "Is she my type or not?"

Carson thought for a moment. Brian liked beautiful women and Libby definitely met his criteria with her dark brown hair, brilliant blue eyes and ivory skin.

But Brian also wanted a woman who liked to party. Though Carson didn't know Libby very well, he knew she worked two jobs. That couldn't leave much time for extracurricular activities.

"No, she's not," Carson said. "I mean she's certainly pretty enough, but she's more the quiet dinner-for-two type than the—"

"Swim-nude-in-the-pool-at-4:00-a.m. type?"

Carson laughed.

"Just give it to me straight." Brian finished off his drink and motioned to the waiter to bring him another. "I can take it."

"She hates you," Carson said.

"She's never even met me," Brian protested.

Carson shrugged and took a sip of his soda.

Brian leaned forward and a knowing look filled his eyes. "I get it now. You're interested in her."

Carson shook his head. "I don't have time for a relationship. You know that."

"Buddy, listen to me. You need to relax." Brian took another sip of his drink. "Live a little."

"There's way too much work to be done around here," Carson said, making no apologies and asking for no sympathy. It had been part of their agreement when they'd first agreed to work together; Brian would furnish the start-up cash and he'd furnish the hard work. "Eventually I'd like the place to be doing well enough that I could afford to expand."

"I've got an easy solution to that problem, and it doesn't involve a lot of work," Brian said. "Forget the waitress. Concentrate on finding a woman with money."

"What are you talking about?"

"Marry someone wealthy." Brian snapped his fingers. "Voilà. Instant capital."

Though Carson had grown up poor, his mother had instilled a strong moral code in all her sons. "I could never use someone that way."

Brian threw a handful of nuts into his mouth and his voice grew louder. "You're not using anyone. You're confining your future wife search to women with money. Didn't your mother teach you that it's just as easy to love a rich woman as a poor one?''

"You're talking crazy, man."

"I'm talking common sense." Brian leaned back in his chair. "If you think about it, you'll realize I'm right."

"Okay, I promise," Carson said, more in an effort to placate Brian than out of any real interest. "Once I finish doing everything I have to do around here and take care of my other obligations, I'll go searching for an heiress to fall in love with."

"Smart man." Brian nodded. "Just keep your eyes open. They're everywhere, though they can be hard to spot. You just have to be alert."

Carson nodded, but his thoughts weren't on faceless rich young women who might walk through his restaurant door someday, but on a certain dark-haired beauty without a cent to her name, who already had.

Chapter Four

Libby waited for the traffic light to change and eyed the Sunrise Coffee Company sign up ahead. Though she was running late for work, she *had* to stop for some espresso. After all, everyone knew caffeine was essential to sound mental functioning. And since this would be her first day on the job after her embarrassing fall, her brain cells needed to be firing on all cylinders.

It didn't help her concentration that she'd stayed up way past midnight watching an old Audrey Hepburn movie on television. When the alarm rang at seven she'd been barely able to pry her eyelids open. In fact she'd thrown the dainty clock across the room without even lifting her head from the pillow. Luckily it was one her mother had sent her from France and she'd never really liked it anyway.

Libby pulled into the parking lot of the coffee shop, surprised to see the lot already filled with cars. Why weren't these people home in bed? That's where she'd be if she hadn't made that crazy deal.

The only open spot was next to a red Jeep, a vehicle that looked surprisingly similar to the one Carson drove. For a brief moment she wondered if it could be his, but then she reminded herself that this was California, the land of cute little SUVs and 4x4s.

Libby wheeled into the parking place, desperately missing her BMW roadster. Unfortunately, because of the switch, Sierra was now driving it while Libby was stuck with a late eighties gas guzzler that didn't even have power windows, much less a CD player.

The sacrifices she's had to make…

Libby shook her head and turned off the ignition, trying not to feel sorry for herself. Perhaps she should splurge and get a scone with her coffee. Maybe that would brighten her spirits.

The dining portion of the coffee shop was filled, but Libby barely gave the crowded tables a second glance. She moved directly to the take-out line in front of the cases of baked goods. Thankfully, there was only one customer in front of her—an older woman with tightly permed hair and oversize glasses.

''Now tell me again the difference between a latte and a cappuccino?'' the woman asked for the second time since Libby had walked up.

Libby glanced at the overhead clock. Ten minutes.

If the woman didn't make up her mind pretty soon, Libby was going to have to order for her. Either that, or risk being late for work.

The college-age clerk and Libby exchanged a smile when the woman finally chose neither a cappuccino or a latte, but rather the house blend and a scone.

"I'll have a tall double espresso," Libby said, fishing the money out of her bag. "And a peach scone."

"I'm sorry." The guy shook his head. "The woman before you got the last one."

"How could you be out already?" Despite her best efforts to control it, Libby's voice rose. "It's not even eight o'clock."

The guy shrugged. "Everybody wanted scones today. Tomorrow it'll be something else. We've got lots of muffins."

"Do you have any in the oven?" Libby asked, clinging to one faint shred of hope.

"Nope," the clerk said, glancing at the growing line behind her. "Look, you still want the espresso or not?"

Libby nodded and rubbed a weary hand across her face. It wasn't the guy's fault she was irritable. If Audrey and what's-his-name had gotten together a little sooner she could have gone to bed at a decent time. Libby shoved a five-dollar bill across the counter and smiled an apology. "Keep the change."

Moving to the side to wait for her drink, Libby

couldn't help but wonder if this was what poor people faced every day: one disappointment after another. And having to get up early to be at work at the crack of dawn was bound to make any disappointment seem even worse.

"Libby." A familiar voice sounded, and Libby whirled.

Carson stood behind her, dressed in khaki shorts and a green polo, an irresistible smile on his face.

Libby glanced down at her own tan-colored shorts and green shirt then back at him. "Team Carson?"

He laughed.

"You have to admit—" she wrinkled her nose "—it has a certain ring to it."

Carson just shook his head and laughed again.

Libby couldn't believe her luck. Running into her new boss couldn't have happened at a better time. Now she didn't have to worry about getting to work. After all, they were talking about his business, so in a way they were already there.

"Your espresso is up," a red-haired woman behind the counter announced, slapping a palm loudly on the counter.

Libby ignored the woman and took the drink, keeping her gaze on Carson. It was crazy. Though she hadn't yet had a single drop of her caffeine-laden drink, Libby suddenly felt wide-awake. "Do you have time to sit and talk?"

"Hmm." A thoughtful look crossed Carson's face.

"I have an employee coming in at eight for office procedures orientation but something tells me she's going to be late."

"She probably doesn't want to appear too eager," Libby said, tossing the words over her shoulder. She crossed the room and took a seat at a table by the window.

"I'm sure you're right," he said, following behind her. "Appearing eager and ready to learn in a new job is the kiss of death."

Libby laughed. "Exactly."

Carson pulled out a chair and took a seat opposite her.

"Aren't you going to have anything to drink?" Libby stared curiously at his empty hands. Carson was one of the few in the place who didn't have a cup of something.

Carson shook his head. "Actually I've been here for the past hour and I'm all coffeed out."

Libby took a sip of espresso and settled back in her chair, suddenly feeling happy. Meeting friends for coffee or drinks was one of her favorite pastimes. "Did you have a meeting?"

"Bible study." Carson placed the book he'd been holding onto the table. Only then did Libby realize the black bound book wasn't the latest murder mystery or medical thriller.

Her smile froze on her lips. "I hope you're not going to try to convert me."

Carson looked askance. ''What?''

''Because you don't need to bother. I already have my own faith,'' she said, using the pat response that had always worked so well in the past when she'd been approached.

''What are you talking about?'' Carson's brows drew together.

''You, going door-to-door in a dark suit trying to convert people.'' Libby gestured toward the Bible. ''I'm telling you up front I don't need to be converted. I'm already a believer.''

It was true but only in the most limited sense of the term.

''Good,'' he said, still looking confused. ''I mean, great. Not that our Bible study goes door-to-door or anything.''

''Some groups do. But I just tell them I have my own faith.'' Libby took a sip of espresso.

''Makes sense.'' Carson stared at her, a puzzled expression still furrowing his brow. ''Where do you attend church?''

Libby thought quickly, which was next to impossible on five hours of sleep and only a sip of caffeine. ''First Christian.''

It was actually Sierra's church, but Libby had attended there with her friend when she was a child and so in a way it was her church, too. And really, did churches belong to anyone but God, anyway?

Carson paused then shook his head. "I don't think I know anyone who goes there."

"I'm not really into talking about my faith," Libby said quickly, in an attempt to make sure he didn't ask her any more questions. "I believe in living it."

Carson nodded. "I've always thought you should be able to tell a Christian by their actions."

Libby met his gaze, amazed they were having this discussion. She'd never really known a man who lived his faith. Her father, what she could remember of him anyway, had a standing golf date every Sunday morning, and none of the men she'd ever dated had ever even mentioned God, unless it was in a curse.

"By the way, how's the arm?" Carson asked suddenly.

A warning shiver traveled up her spine. Though she was glad they weren't talking about God anymore, Libby wasn't sure she wanted to talk about her return to the dining room.

"A little better." She spoke slowly, choosing her words carefully. "But it still hurts when I lift things. I have a feeling it'll be a while before I can carry those heavy trays."

The last impression Libby wanted to convey was that she was ready to wait tables again. Actually she'd be happy if she never took another order. Though it probably wasn't realistic, she couldn't help but hope her stint in the office would work out so well she could stay there permanently. Or, at least until she and Sierra switched back at the end of the summer.

"I don't want you to wait tables until you're completely ready," he said. "So we'll take it slow and *you* tell me when it's all better."

Libby smiled. Though she'd never been a malingerer, she had the feeling that this was one arm that was going to take a long, long time to heal.

"I really thought the label on that French terracotta pot read twenty-five dollars," Sierra said apologetically. She'd stopped at Libby's house to get her signature on some checks and Libby had convinced her to stay for a glass of mango iced tea. They sat on the veranda enjoying the late-afternoon coolness. "When Dottie told me it was two hundred and fifty, I freaked. I'm so sorry, Libby. You can take the difference out of my paycheck."

Libby couldn't help but smile. When she'd first taken over the antique store she hadn't known a Loetz vase from a Lalique. The first week in business she'd let a Tiffany Floriform slip out of the store for a tenth of what it was worth. She waved a hand in the air. "Don't give it another thought. I've made mistakes ten times worse."

"I can't imagine that. You're way too organized." Sierra sighed. "But I'll be more careful, I promise."

"It's okay," Libby said. "Don't sweat it."

"If you say so." Sierra took a sip of tea. "Tell me about your day. Did you enjoy working in the office?"

"Let's just say it was better than waiting tables," Libby said with a grin. "I inputted figures into the computer, formatted a couple of spreadsheets—simple stuff like that. Thankfully the day just flew by."

When five o'clock came Libby had found herself hoping Carson would ask her to stay and have dinner with him. But he'd only thanked her and offered an absentminded smile before turning his attention back to a hostess who'd come to the office with a dining room problem.

Libby wondered if Carson ever got tired of the long hours and all the problems. It had to be hard....

"Libby?"

She jerked her head up to find Sierra staring at her, a tiny smile lifting the corners of her lips. "I said," Sierra repeated, "maybe he'll let you stay and work in the office permanently. It would certainly be easier than being on your feet all day and then all night, too."

"All night?" Libby furrowed her brow. "I don't work at night."

"You don't right now," Sierra explained patiently. "But my mother is catering a lot of parties this summer."

"And that has what to do with me?" Libby shifted

uncomfortably in her chair. The question begged to be asked but Libby had the feeling she didn't want to know the answer.

"Part of taking over my life," Sierra said, "is doing everything I did. And that includes helping my mother with her catering business."

Libby groaned. She vaguely remembered this being part of the agreement. "How many nights?"

"Usually two," Sierra said. "Most of the events are on Friday or Saturday nights."

Libby straightened. "I don't work weekends. I've *never* worked weekends."

"Working when and if you feel like it is the prerogative of the rich." Sierra lifted a brow, an amazing lack of sympathy in her tone. "Poor people usually have to work during the day *and* at night just to make ends meet. And, more often than not they work on the weekends, too. Since you're poor for the summer—"

Sierra let the sentence dangle, unfinished in the air.

The last thing Libby wanted to do was to complete it. But she also knew Sierra was going to sit there with that expectant look on her face until she did.

Libby heaved a resigned sigh. "Since I'm poor I have to work the weekends."

Sierra smiled at Libby's lack of enthusiasm. "I told you I was getting the best part of the bargain. But you didn't believe me."

Though she was beginning to believe it, Libby

wasn't ready to admit that she'd been wrong. After all there had been some good things about the switch—Carson Davies for example. She would have never met him if she hadn't taken Sierra's place at the restaurant. And even though he hadn't asked her out, given time he would.

"I have to admit that working all these hours is a definite minus, but I think being around Carson moves me back into the plus column."

"Carson?" Sierra set down her glass of tea. "The owner?"

Libby rolled her eyes. "How many Carsons do I know?"

"I thought you didn't like him," Sierra said. "That first day you said he was a slave driver."

"I believe I said—" Libby searched her memory for her exact comment "—that he was a slave driver but also a hunk."

Sierra leaned back in her chair and studied Libby thoughtfully. "Okay, then, what about your decision to swear off men?"

Libby widened her eyes. "Swear off men?"

The innocent expression might have fooled someone else, but she and Sierra were as close as sisters.

"Don't even try that," Sierra said. "After you and Stephen broke up, I distinctly remember you telling me you were swearing off men."

Libby nodded, picking up the tiny shortbread

cookie she'd sworn she wasn't going to eat. She took a bite. "So?"

"O-kay." Sierra paused, clearly trying to milk the moment. "Carson is a man, right?"

Libby smiled. Carson wasn't just a man, he was a blond Adonis. Her heart picked up speed at the thought of what it would be like to be ensconced in his strong arms, to feel his warm lips on hers...

Libby shook her head, reminding herself they'd never even been on a date so it was a little early to think about kissing.

"Yes, he's a man," Libby said, when the silence lengthened and she realized Sierra actually expected an answer to her ridiculous question. "But all I'm looking for is some harmless fun, a little holding hands down by the wharf, a few kisses under the stars, stuff like that. Definitely not anything serious."

"Why not?" Sierra asked. "It sounds like he's got a lot going for him. Why wouldn't you be interested?"

"Because the minute I start being interested, it will turn bad. Don't ask me why, it just will," Libby said. "I want to keep it simple. If he likes me and I like him, we go out. I don't spend time obsessing about the future, because I know up front there isn't going to be any between us."

"Do you think that's being fair to him?" A hint of reproach filled Sierra's tone.

"It's a guy's dream," Libby said, keeping her tone

light though she couldn't help but be upset by her friend's unexpected censure. "Anyway, Carson is a workaholic. I'll be lucky to get him to ask me out."

"He'll ask you out," Sierra said.

The bold confidence in Sierra's tone took Libby by surprise. "How can you be so sure?"

"Because you don't really care," Sierra said, lifting one shoulder in a slight shrug. "Indifference is the ultimate aphrodisiac."

Chapter Five

Libby stared at the P&L statement on the screen in front of her. The restaurant was doing surprisingly well considering it had only been open a year.

She was supposed to be keying data into the computer, but her mind kept drifting. Libby glanced at the clock, wondering when Carson was going to return. He'd been there to greet her when she'd cruised through the door at eight-twenty. He'd left shortly after, but not before reminding her that the work day started at eight, not eight-twenty.

Libby hadn't been about to let such a cheap shot go unanswered. She'd informed him that she'd been planning her day while standing in line for a cappuccino. So, in essence, she *was* on time.

He'd laughed as if she were joking.

"What do we have here?"

The deep voice took her by surprise and Libby swiveled in her chair.

A tall, slender man with jet-black hair and golden eyes stood in the doorway, his appreciative gaze lingering on Libby's bare legs before slowly moving up her body to her face.

Not intimidated even by such boldness, Libby stared back. He was dressed in a dark suit, not khakis and a polo shirt, so she knew he wasn't an employee. "May I help you?"

"I'm Brian Reiter," he said, as if that explained everything.

Libby lifted a brow.

"You don't recognize the name?" The man's tone stopped just short of being arrogant.

"Should I?" Libby asked, finding his confidence more appealing than the man himself.

"I own Carson's Waterfront," he said. His gaze flickered from the stack of work piled in front of her on the desk to her khaki shorts and polo. "That makes me your boss."

Libby leaned back in her chair and studied the man. She wasn't sure what kind of game he was playing and she knew she should probably shut him down, but talking to him beat putting numbers into the computer. "I didn't realize this was *Brian*'s Waterfront. For some reason the name *Carson* sticks in my mind."

"Carson?" he asked. "Who's he?"

The twinkle in his eye made it impossible for Libby to keep from smiling.

"You know," she said, "the blond-haired guy who looks as if he should be carrying a surfboard."

Laughter sounded from her left. "I must really project a professional image."

Libby turned to find Carson standing in the back doorway, his arms folded across his chest. Her heart picked up speed, but she kept her tone casual. "I was just talking to the boss-man."

Carson's gaze shifted to Brian. "Boss?"

"Brian tells me he owns the place." Libby widened her eyes. "And he says that makes him my boss."

Carson's eyes darkened.

"Don't shoot. It was just a little joke." Brian held up his hands in mock surrender, then cast a sideways glance at Libby. "Of course, Carson and I are partners. So, in a sense, we're both your boss."

If Libby hadn't been looking directly at Carson she would have missed the quick spark of anger that flared in his eyes then disappeared just as quickly.

"Brian is right," Carson said in an easy, offhand tone. "We are partners. But under our agreement I manage the restaurant and the employees. So, if you have any questions you come to me."

"And if you're interested in going out for dinner, you come to me," Brian said with a leering gaze that was so ridiculous and overdone, Libby had to laugh.

"I'll keep that in mind," she said.

"How about tonight?" Brian asked, his gaze lingering on her bare legs.

Though her khaki shorts hadn't seemed all that short this morning, Libby had to resist the urge to pull them down to cover even more skin.

"She can't," Carson said. "She's busy tonight."

"I am?" Libby tilted her head, fascinated by the undercurrent of tension between the two men.

"I asked a couple of days ago if you'd be free to go over the staff schedules with me," Carson said. "If you've changed your mind…"

"Not at all." Libby racked her brain for that conversation but all she could recall was a brief mention of having her analyze the schedules "sometime soon." She hadn't realized he'd meant tonight. But then, she had a sneaking suspicion he hadn't known it would be tonight, either. "I can work this evening."

If Brian was disappointed, he didn't let it show. He shrugged. "Carson told me you were a hard worker, but it still surprises me that you'd choose work over dinner with me."

"Hmm. Dinner and you? I may have to call in sick." Libby cast a teasing gaze at Carson, pleased to see his expression darken.

"Just kidding." Libby gave Carson a wink before turning back to Brian. "Another time perhaps?"

"You can count on it," Brian said with an easy smile.

Carson muttered something under his breath and his partner laughed.

"Carson, do you have a minute?" Brian asked. "I've got a few business items to discuss."

Carson glanced at the papers Libby had scattered across his desk. "We can meet in the break room. It should be empty."

"I've got an even better idea." Libby pushed her chair back from the desk and stood. "Why don't *I* go there and you two stay here and have your meeting?"

Carson glanced at Brian then back at Libby. "If you're sure you wouldn't mind."

"Hmm." Libby paused for a moment, one finger pressed to her lips. "Would I mind taking a break? No, I'm willing to make the sacrifice."

Carson smiled. "I'll come and get you when we're finished."

"No rush. I need to increase my knowledge of current events and thankfully there's a whole stack of *People* magazines in the break room." Her lips quirked up in a grin.

Carson chuckled.

"It was nice to meet you, Libby," Brian said when she turned to go. "I'll call you."

Libby didn't bother to respond. She knew he wouldn't use the phone. Instead, in about three days

he'd stop by the restaurant and repeat his dinner offer. Then, depending on how she felt at the moment,
she'd say yes or no.

Without a backward glance, Libby moved to the
door. Though the two men had started to talk about
some new clause in their liability insurance even before she was out of the room, Libby could feel their
eyes follow her.

She smiled and let the office door close behind her.

"I can see why you like her." Brian plopped into
the chair next to the desk and leaned back.

Carson rubbed his neck with his hand. The day had
started off badly with a malfunction in one of the
ovens and several staff calling in sick. The problem
with the liability insurance had been icing on the
cake. And now to have to discuss Libby with Brian...

"I don't like her," Carson said finally, pulling out
his leather desk chair and sitting down. "Not in the
way that you mean."

The look in Brian's eyes said he clearly didn't believe Carson, but instead of confronting his friend,
Brian just smiled. "Well, I like her. She has that kind
of classy elegance that has always appealed to me."

Carson lifted a brow. He knew the kind of woman
that appealed to his friend and he couldn't think of
one woman Brian had dated in the past twelve
months who fit that description.

Brian chuckled as if he knew the direction of Carson's thoughts. "I know Sandi and most of the women you've seen me with haven't really fallen into that category but maybe that's why those relationships never lasted."

"So you're saying you think you could be seriously interested in Libby?" Carson couldn't believe his ears.

"I'm not going that far." Brian laughed. "But she's beautiful and there's something about her that intrigues me. Like there's more to her than meets the eye."

Carson knew exactly what his friend was saying. He'd had that same feeling from the moment he'd first seen the woman.

"This thing tonight that you came up with—" Brian paused, gesturing with his hand as if trying to recall Carson's exact words.

"Going over the schedules?" Carson offered.

"That was all a ruse." Brian's lips quirked up in a knowing smile. "To keep her from going out with me."

"I've already told you before, you're not the right type of guy for her," Carson said honestly.

"How do you know that?"

"Because I know her," Carson said. "And, more importantly, I know you."

"It's not just about the physical with me," Brian protested. "I know it may seem that way, but I can be committed. I just have to find the right woman."

"I don't know why we're even talking about this." Carson raked a hand through his hair. "Contrary to what you may think, it doesn't matter to me who you date. Date Libby if you want or don't date her. It doesn't matter to me."

"You might say that," Brian said. "But are you going to have work for her to do every time I ask her out? All I'm saying is if this is all because you want her, just say the word and I'll back off."

As tempting as it was to tell Brian that was the case, Carson couldn't lie. "You know the restaurant keeps me too busy to date. Not to mention Becca and Seth."

Brian waved a dismissive hand. His partner had never understood the obligation Carson felt to Becca. As far as Brian was concerned, when his brother's girlfriend had decided to continue her pregnancy, raising that child was her responsibility. But Seth was Carson's nephew and Becca was the woman his brother had once loved. That made them his family. And one thing Carson had learned from his mother was that families stuck together.

"What about Audra?" Brian asked, lifting a brow. "You went out with her."

"Audra is great." Carson chose his words carefully, knowing Brian and Audra were good friends. "But what we have is a business relationship."

"So you're not going to see her again?" Brian asked, surprise evident in his tone.

Carson pushed the stack of papers sitting in front of him to the side. "Actually, I'm seeing her tonight."

"Tonight?" Brian's gaze narrowed. "You're going to be busy, yet you torpedo my plans with Libby under the guise of working on those schedules."

"Audra and I aren't going out until after nine," Carson repeated. "Libby and I will be done way before then."

"I have to hand it to you." Unexpected admiration filled Brian's tone. "You knew Libby could have still gone out with me. But you said nothing."

Carson shrugged.

"Dating two women in one night." Brian shook his head. "I'm proud of you, boy."

"Knock it off, Brian," Carson growled. "Both of these 'dates' are work related and you know it."

Brian tilted his head and stared at Carson for a long moment. "You know Audra's father owns Pacific Meats."

"I know that," Carson said. "His company is one of the largest distributors of organic meat in this part of the country."

"Now it's finally all making sense." Brian's smile widened. "I'm glad to hear you finally decided to heed my advice."

"What advice?"

"That you should find yourself an heiress. I have to admit I never thought you'd actually do it." Brian laughed. "I guess I was wrong."

Chapter Six

Libby left the office at three, promising Carson she'd return around seven to go over the schedules. Once she got home she crashed, falling asleep the second her head hit the pillows. Ever since college she'd been addicted to afternoon naps.

By the time Libby woke, it was after six and she scurried to get ready. Taking a quick shower, she reapplied her makeup and hurriedly curled her hair. But, though she tried to tell herself that tonight was all business, Libby couldn't bring herself to pull on those khaki shorts and that horrid polo.

Instead she opted for a white eyelet sundress that accentuated her tan and made her dark hair look almost black. When she'd tried it on in the store, Sierra had told her she looked like a model, all lean and alluring. Of course, she'd had to buy it.

Libby spritzed on a few drops of her favorite perfume, a light airy fragrance that reminded her of springtime.

Though on the surface Carson seemed like an all-work-and-no-play kind of guy, the look in his eyes this afternoon told her that tonight might not be all business.

The drive to the restaurant should have been pleasant, but the air conditioner on the Buick conked out halfway across town. Libby had no choice but to roll down the windows. By the time she pulled into the parking lot, her once-lovely hair was a mass of tangled curls.

But the moment she stepped out of the car her mood lifted and a shiver of anticipation raced up her spine. Tonight she'd be spending the evening with a man who'd captured her interest the moment she'd first laid eyes on him. She felt like a teenager again, taking it a night at a time, not giving a thought to the future.

Libby walked toward the brightly lit building, a quivery feeling in the pit of her stomach.

Would Carson try to kiss her tonight? Or would he be in his "boss" mode and act as if she was just another employee? She smiled at the parking attendant and walked through the restaurant's front door, eager to have her questions answered.

Libby smiled when Carson greeted her in a pair of navy pants and a button-down shirt, instead of his standard work attire. They talked for a few minutes about the schedules, then he asked if she was hungry.

Now they were sitting in a little Mexican restaurant down the road, drinking margaritas and waiting for their food.

"We could have eaten at the restaurant." Carson grabbed a chip from the basket on the table. "But I think it's good to scout the competition."

"I do, too," Libby concurred, taking a sip of her fruity drink. But she suspected the real reason Carson had suggested they go elsewhere had nothing to do with competition and everything to do with privacy.

Carson knew as well as she did that if they ate at the restaurant, the employees would watch every move and listen to every word.

He finished the chip then reached for another. "So, do you think you'll go out with Brian if he calls?"

There existed the slight possibility that Carson was asking on Brian's behalf, trying to save his friend the embarrassment of asking if she planned on saying no anyway. But Libby had the feeling that this question was for Carson's edification, not to help out his business associate.

"I don't know," Libby said honestly. She took a chip from the wicker basket and dipped it into the salsa. "It depends."

Carson lifted a brow and brought the drink to his lips. "On what?"

"On a lot of things," she said. "On how he asks,

on how I feel that day, on whether on not there's anything going on between you and me.''

Carson choked on his drink, bringing a napkin to his lips.

She munched on the chip, giving him time to regain his composure.

''We work together,'' he said finally. ''There can't be anything between you and me.''

Libby stared at him for a long moment. Men could be such stupid creatures. Like Carson now, pretending he didn't want to date her. The only one he was fooling was himself.

''Okay,'' Libby said, lifting her shoulder in a careless shrug. ''Then I guess my decision to go out with Brian will just depend on how he asks and if I feel like saying yes that day.''

''Brian is a nice guy,'' Carson said. ''And a close friend.''

''Great.'' Libby grabbed another chip and glanced around the restaurant, checking out the other diners.

''But that said, I have to tell you that Brian isn't what he seems,'' Carson said.

Libby pondered Carson's words for moment, wondering if he was really making any sense. ''He's not a guy?''

Carson chuckled. ''Of course he's a guy.''

''He's not friendly?''

''Actually, that's one of the problems.'' Carson

leaned forward, resting his arms on the table. "Sometimes he can be a little too friendly."

"Hmm." Libby bit her cheek to keep from smiling at his serious, paternalistic tone. But like the defiant teenager she'd once been, she cocked a quizzical brow and pretended not to understand. "That doesn't make sense. How can a person be too friendly?"

Carson groaned and sat back. "You're not making this easy."

Libby merely smiled and took a sip of her drink.

"All right, I'm going to just say it straight out— Brian is a player," Carson said. "He likes women for only one thing. If that's the kind of relationship you want, then he's your man."

His chin lifted and Libby could feel him practically daring her to say she was so shallow that's all she wanted. But though it was fun to tease him, she wasn't sixteen and this time she had to be honest.

"Recently I dated a guy whom I thought might be the one." Her thoughts returned to those first few months after she'd met Stephen. "From the very start he made it clear he wanted me. I told him I wanted to wait and he seemed okay with it, but he didn't wait. He just turned to someone else, but forgot to tell me about it."

Normally Libby liked to keep her personal affairs private. She didn't know why she was telling Carson all this, unless it was some deep-seated need to make it absolutely clear that a man like Brian Reiter wasn't her type.

"What a jerk," Carson said.

"He never loved me." Disappointment colored Libby's words. "The only thing he loved was my money."

"Your money?" Carson's brow furrowed. "I got the impression you lived paycheck to paycheck."

Libby froze, cursing her carelessness. Now she had only seconds to pull herself out of the hole she'd dug. She thought quickly.

"I'm talking future income." She fluttered one hand in the air. "Stephen thought because I was getting my college degree that I was headed for the big time."

Carson covered her hand with his. "You're better off without someone like that. One of these days you'll find the right man. He'll appreciate all your wonderful qualities and won't care if you're rich or poor."

"The funny thing is I don't even miss Stephen," Libby said. "I think I was more in love with the idea of being in love than I was in love with him." She paused for a moment. "Does that make sense?"

Carson's lips quirked in a smile. "I hate to say it, but it does."

"I guess what I'm trying to say is that I'm not interested in dating another man with those same characteristics," Libby said.

"That's why I said something," Carson said. "I like Brian, but I don't want him fooling with your head. You're too nice a person for that."

"You think I'm nice?" Libby gazed up at him through lowered lashes, her heart picking up speed.

"You're *very* nice," Carson said softly. Leaning forward, he reached over and caressed her cheek with the back of his hand. "And incredibly beautiful."

From the time she'd been thirteen and had outgrown the childish gangliness, Libby had heard those words more times than she could count. But somehow they sounded different coming from Carson's lips.

"Excuse me, sir." The waiter's voice sounded from behind Libby.

Carson immediately pulled back his hand, and the warmth that had started to flood through Libby's body came to an abrupt halt. Reluctantly she sat back, allowing the waiter to place a taco salad in front of her.

She lifted her fork and stared down at the food, suddenly no longer hungry.

"Something wrong?" Carson paused, fork in hand. His eyes filled with concern.

How could she tell him that disappointment had stolen her appetite? That she knew he was so close to kissing her that she could practically taste his lips on hers? That the thing that she wanted most at this moment wasn't food, but him?

But she couldn't tell him any of those things, so she brought up the first thing that popped into her mind. "I was just thinking how much food we have in this country. And how much of it ends up in a Dumpster at the end of the evening."

Last night, a local television station's camera crew had caught a bag lady scrounging through the garbage behind a restaurant in downtown Santa Barbara. The sight of the woman with her head in the Dumpster and only her bare legs visible had made Libby pause in front of the TV set. She'd stayed for a few minutes longer listening to civic leaders debate the homeless issue. But when she realized they weren't going to show how the woman got out of the trash, Libby had flipped off the set.

Carson took a bite of his cheese enchilada. "You're right. And, as a Christian, I find it hard to believe that we can't find a way to ensure the neediest among us don't go hungry."

"The mayor said he wished more of the restaurants would donate their leftovers to the homeless shelters." Libby stabbed a piece of lettuce with her fork, wondering if the shelter residents ever got tired of eating leftover restaurant food. Of course, she reminded herself, compared to what that woman found in the Dumpster, anything would have to be an improvement.

"We donate to the shelters," Carson said matter-of-factly, reaching for another chip.

"You do?" Libby didn't even know why she was surprised. If anyone would donate, it would be Carson.

Carson nodded. "Like you, throwing away good food makes me sick to my stomach."

Actually it was the thought of that woman crawling through the garbage that made Libby sick to her stomach. But she did agree with Carson. Throwing away something perfectly useful made no sense.

"How does that work?" Libby asked, dumping a dollop of the salsa on her salad. "How do you know the food gets where it needs to go?"

"Erin takes care of all that," Carson said.

A picture of the perky redhead Libby had met the first day on the job flashed through her mind. "But she's only a high school student. Isn't that a lot of responsibility for someone so young?"

"She's not really that young." Carson laughed. "Actually Erin is a student at City College. She just looks like she's—"

"Sixteen." Libby filled in the blank and they exchanged a smile.

"She's done a good job with the program," Carson said. "A really good job."

For a second Libby wondered if that was more than admiration in his tone or if he was one of those men who liked redheads. But she shoved the jealous thought aside before it could take hold.

"She seems very organized," Libby said. "And

she's really personable. Both of those qualities would be assets in that position.''

Carson stared at Libby thoughtfully for a moment. ''You're personable. And organized.''

Libby smiled, pleased that he'd noticed what so many men failed to see—that she had a brain in addition to passably good looks. She wondered if it was the way she'd reorganized his files or the spreadsheets she'd set up that gave him his first clue that she was organized. And, as far as the personable part, Libby had been able to talk to anybody about anything since her first words had left her mouth. ''Thank you. That's nice of you to say.''

''I didn't say it to be nice.''

Libby leaned back in her chair and tilted her head. ''Don't tell me you want something from me?''

Carson laughed. ''Actually I do.''

A shiver of anticipation shot up her spine. She placed her fork back on the table. ''You've got my full attention.''

Chapter Seven

Though Libby usually read men like a book, she didn't have a clue what Carson was going to say next.

"I don't know if Erin told you much about her summer plans?"

Her heart plummeted. He wanted to talk about Erin?

"When we were together we talked mostly about work," Libby said. "There wasn't much time for personal stuff."

"Then this probably isn't making much sense." Carson shot her an apologetic look. "Let me explain. Erin is going to Europe on an exchange program for the rest of the summer."

"How fun." Libby's mother had been living in France the last ten years, and although they'd never been close, Libby had always enjoyed visiting her mother in Paris. She started to tell Carson that if Erin had any questions, she'd love to help her out, but she came to her senses just in time.

Carson thought she was a starving college student. The last she knew poor people didn't frequent the Riviera or the Monte Carlo casinos or know the best dance clubs in Italy. They worked day and night, and if they were lucky they went to Reno once a year for the weekend.

Libby shuddered at the thought. Maybe Sierra had been right. Maybe it was better to be rich. Still, she really hadn't given this being poor thing a fair trial. And there had certainly been some good things to come out of this experience. She sipped her drink and stared at Carson through lowered lashes.

"I was thinking you'd be perfect for the job," he said.

"Job?" Libby widened her gaze and straightened in her seat. The last thing she needed was more work. "What are you talking about?"

"I'd like you to take over Erin's duties."

Libby started shaking her head even before he finished speaking. Between this job and the catering stuff, she'd be working almost forty hours. A woman could only do so much. Especially a woman who'd always believed a three-day workweek was more than enough. "Thanks for the offer but I simply can't add one more thing to my plate."

Surprise skittered across Carson's face. "But you'd be perfect for it."

Libby couldn't argue with that fact, but the issue wasn't whether she was suited to the position, but if she had the time. "It sounds very interesting but with waiting tables…"

"What would you think about not going back to waiting tables at all? Instead you could split your time helping me in the office and coordinating the food donations," Carson said. "It would look good on a résumé."

Libby laughed at his persuasive tone and enticing smile. Though she was sorely tempted to take him up on the offer, she couldn't. Sierra was counting on the money Libby would make in tips to help with her fall tuition.

"I agree that it would look good on a résumé, but if I don't finish college I won't need a résumé." Libby sighed. "And right now I need the tip money more than I need the experience."

"You're probably right," Carson said thoughtfully, watching a waiter at a nearby table pocket a twenty-dollar bill. "I know the servers at the Waterfront make great tips, especially on the weekend."

Libby forced a brave smile. From the very beginning, Libby had wanted to just write Sierra a check, but her stubborn friend insisted that Libby had to earn the money. According to her friend, in order to understand how the other half lived, she needed to "walk a mile in their shoes." That meant doing things like working at a job you didn't particularly like, because it paid more.

"Libby."

Libby lifted her gaze to find Carson staring at her. Her heart picked up speed at the look in his eye.

"I've got a proposition for you."

Libby swallowed hard, her throat suddenly dry. She lifted the glass to her lips and let the cool fruity beverage slide down her throat.

"I've been thinking." He pushed aside his plate of enchiladas as if they were cluttering his thoughts as well as the table. "What if we figured up what you'd make in tips and adjusted your salary accordingly? Then would you accept my offer?"

Libby wanted to say yes, but she'd learned long ago to proceed with caution when something sounded too good to be true. She tilted her head. "Now why would you do that?"

Carson laughed. "I know it doesn't make any business sense. But there were a lot of people who gave me a helping hand when I was just getting started. And this would be a good opportunity for you. Plus I know that I can count on you to do a good job."

Libby stared at him for a long moment. After her previous experiences with men, she couldn't help but be suspicious. It was difficult to believe that any businessman would do something like this just out of the goodness of his heart. Still, Carson seemed sincere and the thought of going back to waiting tables was enough of a reason to give him the benefit of the doubt.

"I'd love to do it," she said with a decisive nod of her head.

He reached over and squeezed her hand. "I'm glad."

She met his gaze and her breath caught in her throat. For a moment the noise of the crowded restaurant dimmed. His eyes drew her in and, though she hadn't moved, it was as if she were drowning in the liquid-blue depths. An intense longing filled every fiber of her being and an answering spark resonated in his gaze. He leaned closer and she followed his direction, her lips tingling with anticipation.

"Would either of you care for dessert this evening?"

Libby jerked back, her gaze seeking the intrusive voice that had popped out of nowhere.

The waiter stood next to the table holding the dessert tray. Though dessert was normally Libby's favorite part of the meal, she barely gave the items a second glance.

"Libby?" Carson raised a brow.

"Not for me, thanks." She was still hungry for something sweet, but not for a Key Lime Costata or Très Leches cake. Her gaze shifted to the glass lining the entire front of the restaurant. Through the large windows Libby could see the lights from a full moon shining on the water. Maybe she'd be able to interest Carson in taking a walk along the beach before they headed back to the Waterfront....

"I'll pass, too," Carson said. He took the check from the waiter and glanced down at his watch. Immediately, he pushed back his chair and stood. "I didn't realize it was this late. We'd better hurry or I won't have time to get you oriented."

"We've got plenty of time." Libby slowly rose to her feet, wondering if this would be the right time to mention the moonlit walk.

"Not really." Carson pulled several bills from his pocket and dropped them on the table along with the check. "I have to be out of the office by nine at the latest."

"Why so early?" Libby shot him a teasing glance. "Do you turn into a pumpkin if you stay out too late?"

Carson laughed and took her arm. "Nothing like that."

"What then?" Libby tilted her head and raised a finger to her lips. "Getting another tattoo on your chest?"

Her words had the desired effect. Carson stopped short, giving her his full attention. "I don't have *any* tattoos anywhere on my body."

The expression on his face made her laugh. Libby thought about asking him to prove it, but decided they hadn't known each other that long and he might think she was serious.

"Okay, then," she said. "What's the rush?"

He cast a sideways glance and reached for the door. "I have a date."

Chapter Eight

Though Libby's smile didn't waver, Carson could see he'd surprised her. He hadn't wanted to blurt it out—in fact he hadn't planned to mention it at all— but she'd backed him into a corner and he wasn't about to lie.

"Who is she?" Libby's voice was amazingly casual and for a second he wondered if he'd imagined the shock in her eyes.

He shrugged. "A friend of Brian's."

"Hmm." A knowing look filled Libby's eyes. "You're dating a friend of Brian's."

It wasn't so much *what* Libby said as *how* she said it. Carson didn't like the look or the insinuation. "What do you mean by that?"

"Nothing." Her eyes widened innocently. "I just

didn't realize that you and Brian shared the same taste in woman, that's all.''

''Not that it's any of your business.'' Carson used the same no-nonsense tone he used with difficult employees, ''But Audra and Brian have never dated.''

Libby smiled politely and walked through the door leading to the parking lot.

''They haven't.''

''I believe you.'' Her voice was sugary sweet.

It didn't fool him a bit.

''Well it's true, whether you choose to believe it or not.'' Hurt made Carson's voice harsh. Granted, he and Libby hadn't known each other long, but he thought she knew him better than that. ''Anyway, I don't see where it's any of your concern.''

Libby's blue eyes widened and two spots of color dotted her cheeks. Carson cursed his impulsivity and his brusqueness.

But before he had a chance to apologize, Libby spoke, her lips curving up in a tight smile. ''You're so right. I'm your employee. You're my boss. It's none of my concern.''

She crossed the street and headed in the direction of the Waterfront. Though her sandals appeared to be more decorative than serviceable, she walked at such a fast clip that Carson was forced to run to catch up.

''Look.'' He grabbed her arm and spun her around. ''I'm sorry. I didn't mean that the way it sounded.''

For a second a spark of anger flashed in her eyes, only to vanish behind a polite mask.

"Don't apologize." She pulled her arm back in a slow deliberate movement. "Like I said, you were right. I was out of line. Who you date is none of my business."

She was upset and he knew that anything he said would only fuel the situation so they walked the rest of the way to the Waterfront in silence. Once they were back in the office, the training moved quickly forward.

Carson would have never gotten through the content if he hadn't known it so well. His concentration was shot. All he could think about was Libby and the laughter they'd shared over dinner and what he could do to bring the smile back to her eyes.

But the opportunity to talk on a personal level never came up. Libby had no trouble mastering the scheduling program and just by the questions she asked he could see she had a good head for business. It was only eight-thirty when they finished.

Instead of lingering to talk, Libby cast a quick glance at the clock and rose to her feet.

Carson stood and awkwardly searched for something to say to ease the newfound tension between them. "Libby—"

"If I leave now, I should still have time—" She reached for her bag, but her hand nervously brushed against a stack of papers on the edge of the desk and sent them fluttering to the floor. Libby hurriedly picked them up and shoved them into his hands. "I need to get going."

Carson frowned. Could Libby have other plans for the evening? He opened his mouth, but shut it without asking.

Like she said, he was her boss.

She was his employee.

And her personal life was none of his business.

The minute Libby arrived home she headed straight upstairs to her bedroom. Tossing the white sundress on the bed, she yanked on a pair of shorts and a tiny tee. She still couldn't believe that an evening that had started out so well had ended so badly. Up until the moment that Carson had dropped that bombshell about having a date, everything had been going fine.

She shook her head. What a fool she'd been. When she'd seen him dressed up, she'd assumed he'd done it for her benefit. Instead, it was for *Audra's* benefit.

Libby paused. There was something naggingly familiar about the name. Finally, an image of a slender woman with a chin-length blond bob flashed before her. The Audra she was thinking of was relatively new to Santa Barbara. And though Libby was sure they'd been at some of the same parties, they'd never been introduced.

Will he kiss her?

Libby shoved the thought aside as of no consequence and headed for the kitchen, her bare feet slapping against the polished hardwood. She opened the refrigerator and stared inside before letting the door fall shut. Though it had to be close to eighty degrees outside, a soothing cup of hot tea still sounded better than a soda. Actually, a scotch on the rocks sounded the best but Libby's mother had been overly fond of medicating her emotions with the stuff and Libby refused to fall into that trap.

After sticking a cup of water in the microwave, Libby grabbed a chamomile tea bag and a box of vanilla wafers from under the counter. By the time the water was heated, she had everything ready on the veranda. She placed the tea and cookies on the small table next to her favorite chair and took a seat on the covered porch. The scent of newly mown grass mixed with the fragrance of a dozen variety of roses.

It was all so familiar. Sometimes Libby felt as if she'd spent half her life sitting alone in the darkness. When she'd been about twelve, she'd been fearful of being in the big house by herself. So when her mother was out for the evening, instead of waiting for her inside, Libby would sit out on the porch steps. But sometimes the sun would be rising in the sky and Libby would still be on the steps.

That's when Peggy had intervened. The housekeeper had insisted Libby spend these lonely evenings with her. Peggy and her daughter, Sierra, had quickly become Libby's surrogate family. And when her mother had married again and decided to move to France when Libby was fifteen, Libby had stayed in Santa Barbara with them.

Her father hadn't been a factor. He'd been out of the picture ever since Libby was ten and her mother had found him in bed with another woman. Stella Carlyle had paid him a healthy sum to get out of her life. The only problem was he'd not only left behind a wife but a daughter, as well.

Libby leaned back in her chair, an unexpected tightness gripping her throat. But she refused to let the tears fall. It didn't matter that her father had left, or that her mother rarely called or visited. Or that Carson Davies had a girlfriend. She didn't need anyone. All she needed was herself.

I will never leave or forsake you.

Libby shook her head vigorously, trying to dislodge the verse. Maybe she should have had the scotch after all. Obviously the tea wasn't strong enough to keep those ridiculous Bible verses from popping into her head. It was those years of Sunday school with Sierra coming back to haunt her.

Sierra might trust in God's promises, but as far as Libby was concerned, the Bible was just a bunch of words. Just like this verse. God had never left her because He'd never been there for her in the first place.

Libby wiped a tear from the corner of her eye and drew a ragged breath. All these years she'd gone it alone. And it had been her own inner strength that had gotten her through the hard times, not some pie-in-the-sky God.

And it would be that same inner strength that would get her through the rest of her life, one day at a time.

"I don't know, Audra." Carson hesitated and leaned back against the park bench, the June sun warming his face. "Saturday nights are crazy at the restaurant. I usually end up putting out one fire after another."

"I know you think they can't do it without you, but I learned a long time ago that no one is indispensable." Audra pushed a strand of short blond hair behind her ear and crossed one shapely leg over the other. "Anyway that's what supervisors and cell phones are for. They handle the little things, and if something big like an earthquake hits, they call you and you say do your best because you can't do anything anyway."

Carson couldn't help but chuckle. Though he wasn't physically attracted to Audra, she did have a quirky sense of humor that he found refreshing.

That's why when she'd called that morning and asked if he wanted to meet her for an early lunch at the park, he'd said yes. He liked her as a person and couldn't think of one reason not to meet her.

But now it seemed he'd opened the door. They'd barely finished their brown bag lunches when she'd asked him to accompany her to an upscale party in Montecito Saturday night.

"There will be lots of people for you to meet...important and influential people," Audra added in a persuasive tone, apparently noticing his hesitation. "In fact, I know for a fact that Rand Dawson from the mayor's office will be there. As the mayor's chief of staff, he has a lot of say in who gets appointed to that new task force."

Carson swallowed the no that had been poised on the tip of his tongue. Audra's suggestion made sense. Granted, there was nothing stopping him from going down to city hall, introducing himself and offering to serve on that new task force. But how far would he get?

He was enough of a realist to know that meeting Rand in a social setting and talking business over drinks and hors d'oeuvres would be the best way of increasing his chances of getting appointed to the new business development task force.

And without some kind of inside pull, Carson knew he stood little chance of being offered a spot. Audra's family, although relatively new in town, had quickly become part of the inner circle of a group of wealthy Santa Barbara business leaders. A few personal introductions from her would go a long way.

But as tempting as it was to further his professional agenda, Carson refused to let Audra think he had romantic feelings toward her. "Audra, I like you, I really do. I think we could be good friends. But as far as there being anything more—"

"Oh, for goodness' sake, Carson, I'm not after your body *or* your heart." Audra rolled her eyes. "I just want a good-looking date for the party."

Another man might have been offended by her bluntness, but Carson felt only a sense of relief. Now, there was nothing standing in the way of him going to the function other than his business. And Audra was right; there was no reason they couldn't get along for one night.

"I'd love to go with you," he said.

"You won't regret it. We'll have a fabulous time," Audra grabbed her purse and stood. "I need to run. Pick me up at seven."

She started down the stepping-stone path then stopped and turned abruptly. "Did I mention it's black-tie?"

Carson smiled. "You just did."

A businessman at a bench down the path lowered his paper and watched appreciatively as she walked by. With her long legs, beautiful face and silver-blond hair, Audra was a striking sight.

Carson knew there were dozens of men who would

give anything to be the man at her side. But her beauty left him cold. Even the emerald-green eyes that everyone always commented on seemed to him to be nothing out of the ordinary.

Though he'd always liked blondes, lately Carson had found himself leaning more to brunettes. Brunettes with beautiful blue eyes.

Chapter Nine

Libby helped Peggy carry the collection of special utensils the woman used for her catering business toward the large hacienda-style home that sat on the edge of Montecito.

Though Libby hadn't had any plans for the evening, she still couldn't believe she was working on a Saturday night. Especially after she'd already put in a full workweek.

"It's so much fun having you here with me." Peggy's brown eyes danced with excitement and Libby couldn't help but smile back.

The trim stylish woman in her early fifties had been Libby's second mother when she was growing up. More than once Libby had told her own mom she wished she'd been Peggy's daughter, not hers.

Libby could still remember the look on her

mother's face. At the time Libby had been glad her words hurt. That's why she'd said them. Though it had taken years, Libby now understood that beneath her mother's self-absorption was a woman who really did love her only child. But back then Libby had been hurt and angry. Hurt over being ignored and angry at a parent who always seemed to prefer her latest boyfriend's company to that of her daughter.

Libby exhaled a heavy sigh. Over the years she'd learned to deal with her mother's attitude, but it still hurt. And, at times, it still made her angry.

"Libby?"

Libby jerked her gaze to Peggy.

Concern furrowed Peggy's brow. "Everything okay?"

Libby could feel her face warm, but she kept her voice light and offhand as she lifted one shoulder in a casual shrug. "I was just thinking about my mom."

Peggy smiled understandingly. She'd worked for Stella Carlyle for almost fifteen years and if anyone knew the woman's good and bad points, it was Peggy. "It's been a while since you've seen her."

Libby's smile never wavered. "A year last Christmas. She thought she might make it back this summer but Jean-Claude wants to go to Greece instead."

"Jean-Claude?" Peggy rolled the name around on her tongue. "Is that the same one she started dating right after she and husband number three split?"

"That was Luc," Libby said with a smile, finding

it humorous that Peggy had forgotten Richard, Stella's third husband's name. "Luc lasted about eight months. Mother says her only consolation was she dumped him before he dumped her."

Peggy chuckled. "That sounds like Stella. I don't know how she maintains such a positive attitude."

"She's philosophical," Libby said. "She says having people be nice to her just because of her money goes with the territory."

"Territory?"

"Being an heiress." Libby lugged a bag of surprisingly heavy cutlery up the back steps of the house, feeling less like an heiress with each step. "You'd be surprised how money colors relationships. You never quite know if someone likes you for who you are or for what you have. That's what I like about Sierra and I trading places—it's me they'll either like or dislike now."

"Not all people are so shallow," Peggy protested.

"Not all," Libby said with a half laugh, not surprised at Peggy's naiveté. "Just most. Especially men."

Peggy paused and stared curiously at Libby. "Sierra tells me your boss at the restaurant is very good-looking."

"Carson is handsome," Libby admitted, an image of bright blue eyes and golden blond hair flashing before her. The man was gorgeous, no doubt about it. "But he's not interested in me."

Peggy's eyes widened. "Is he crazy?"

Libby laughed at the shock in her friend's voice. She shook her head.

"Gay?"

Libby smiled. "No way."

"Blind?"

"Peggy, stop." Libby laughed again. "Carson is a normal, heterosexual male with twenty-twenty vision who just happens to not be interested. But that's okay because I'm not interested in him, either."

It was a lie, but she sounded sincere.

"The right one will come along." Peggy opened the back door and held it for Libby. "One of these days."

"Maybe, but I'm not holding my breath." Libby glanced around the kitchen, amazed at the amount of supplies already on the counter. "How many are going to be at this party tonight?"

"Mrs. St. James called it a 'small intimate affair,'" Peggy said. "In catering terms I'm planning for about fifty."

It didn't sound like very many to Libby, but it still took the next two hours to prepare platters of appetizers and desserts for the intimate few. Thankfully the kitchen was a caterer's dream with several commercial ovens, a huge refrigerator and a large expanse of work space.

Though Libby was no culinary genius, she'd helped Peggy in the kitchen more than a few times when she'd been growing up, and they worked well together. Some of her most pleasant memories were of snapping beans or dicing tomatoes while Peggy put the finishing touches on the evening meal. For a moment Libby could almost pretend they were back home laughing and talking. The only thing that ruined the fantasy was the black dress and white apron Peggy had insisted she wear tonight.

All of Peggy's staff were required to wear uniforms. Though Libby's job tonight was supposed to be in the kitchen, Peggy insisted she dress as if she would be serving. Peggy said she'd learned the hard way to always be prepared.

A sigh of relief escaped Libby's lips as the last batch of appetizers came out of the oven. The catering business reminded her of waiting tables; in both jobs you were on your feet way too much.

Libby added garnish to an appetizer tray and placed it out on the counter for Chloe, one of the two college student employees, to take to the guests.

But when Chloe came through the doorway, the girl ignored the tray entirely. "Mrs. Summers?"

"Chloe?" Peggy's voice was filled with concern. "What's wrong?"

Libby shifted her gaze.

"I have a migraine." Chloe's voice trembled as she sank into a nearby chair, cradling her head in her hands. "I took some pills before I came but they haven't helped. It's getting worse."

Peggy pulled out a chair and took a seat next to the girl. "Honey, you need to go home and rest."

Chloe lifted her gaze, her skin pale. She winced against the bright kitchen light. "I don't think I can drive."

"Nina rode with you, right?" Peggy asked.

Chloe nodded.

"Then Nina can drive you home," Peggy said.

"But, Mrs. Summers, the party is just getting started."

"You let me worry about that," Peggy said softly.

"But—"

"Chloe." Though still soft, Peggy's voice had that motherly firmness Libby remembered so well. "Libby and I have it covered."

"We do?" The words popped out of Libby's mouth before she could stop them. Though she knew Peggy was trying to be positive, they were working with a minimal staff. If both girls left, there was no one to fill in.

"Libby will take your place."

"Me?" Libby's voice squeaked. She wanted to help, she really did. But she'd planned to help in the kitchen, not out among the guests. "You know I'm no good at being a server. I told you what happened at the Waterfront."

Peggy smiled reassuringly. "This is much simpler than waiting tables."

"I can show you." Chloe started to stand, then dropped onto the chair, wincing from the pain.

"It's under control." Libby rose and headed for the door. "I graduated summa cum laude from Princeton. I think I can figure this out."

But the moment Libby stepped out of the kitchen her heart picked up speed. She'd hoped to see only a few people milling about, but the small intimate affair spilled out from a large main room into several smaller side rooms and onto a large deck that ran the entire back length of the house.

Lucky for her, though there was a bar outside as well as inside, the elaborately decorated tables holding the appetizers and desserts were confined to the great room.

Although Libby recognized the faces of many of the attendees, she breathed a sigh of relief when she realized there was no one she knew well. And, as she moved about the room checking the appetizer trays and picking up discarded plates, she realized that no one really looked at her. And, even if they gave her more than a cursory glance, all they'd see was a woman with her hair pulled back, dressed in a simple black uniform with the name Sierra stitched above the left pocket in perfectly arched white letters.

Libby returned to the kitchen several times for more appetizer trays. She smiled in satisfaction as she placed another batch of crab-stuffed mushrooms on the serving table closest to the deck. If the way the guests were eating was any indication, Peggy's catering was a big hit.

She gave the silver platter a quarter-degree turn. Satisfied with the table's appearance, Libby turned, ready to head back to the kitchen. But she moved too quickly and her toe caught the table leg. She cried out, and though she struggled to keep her footing, she knew she would have fallen if not for a pair of strong arms that grabbed her at the last minute.

"Thank you so much." Still breathless and trembling, Libby lifted her gaze to the Good Samaritan.

Carson's eyes widened momentarily before he burst into laughter. "When I saw a woman start to fall, I should have guessed it would be you."

Libby couldn't help but laugh with him. "I keep trying to tell everyone I'm a klutz, but no one believes me."

"If you're a klutz—" Carson's gaze lingered on her face and his voice turned husky "—you're a beautiful one."

Strands of hair had come loose and Libby resisted the urge to push them out of her face. She shifted uncomfortably from one foot to another, wishing he'd caught her wearing something other than black polyester.

Because Carson looked splendid. His blond hair was a perfect foil for his tux. And, Libby wasn't sure if it was her imagination but his eyes seemed an even deeper blue this evening.

"I didn't know you were—" they said in unison.

"I didn't know you were—" Libby stopped and laughed.

"I never expected to see you here tonight," Carson said with a lazy smile. But when his gaze slid from her face to take in her dress, apron and serviceable shoes, his brow furrowed. "Why are you dressed like that?"

"I thought it was a costume party and I came as a maid." Libby kept her expression serious and waved a hand in the direction of the front door. "My feather duster is in the car."

For a split second she had him, but then a light of awareness flashed in his eyes.

"So, Sierra." He tilted his head, reading the name from her dress. "Is this what you do when you're not at the Waterfront?"

"A girl has to find fun where she can," Libby said in a flippant tone. "How about you?"

Carson smiled, showing a mouthful of perfect white teeth. "Actually, this is—"

"Miss." A distinguished-looking older woman whom Peggy had pointed out earlier as Mrs. St. James stopped next to Libby. "We're getting very low on desserts and there are some dishes over there that need to be cleared away."

The hostess didn't apologize to Carson for the interruption and Libby flushed at the woman's preemptory tone. She opened her mouth then closed it, reminding herself that she wasn't here as a guest. She was here to work, and Peggy's business reputation was at stake. Good recommendations from customers weren't just nice, they were essential.

"I'm so sorry, ma'am." Libby offered the woman an apologetic look and resisted the ridiculous urge to curtsy. "I'll take care of that right away."

Libby flashed Carson a polite, impersonal smile. "If there's anything else I can do for you, Mr. Davies, don't hesitate to ask."

With those final words, Libby squared her shoulders and headed straight for the kitchen, stopping to pick up a large tray filled with half-empty cups and glasses.

Her priority tonight was doing what she could to ensure that Peggy's catering was a success. That meant all distractions, including Carson Davies, had to be ignored. Libby had the sinking feeling that was going to be the hardest job of all.

Carson watched Libby gather up the dirty dishes, wishing he could carry the heavy tray back to the kitchen for her. It wasn't his style to let others wait on him, but he knew if he did help, Mrs. St. James might think Libby couldn't handle the job. Still, there had to be something…

"Mrs. St. James." Carson extended his hand. "I'm not sure if you remember me. Carson Davies? I own a restaurant in Santa Barbara."

"Of course I remember you, Mr. Davies." Eleanora St. James smiled and took his hand. "We met at the Swanson party a couple of months ago. I was so pleased when my niece told me she was going to be introducing you to some of her contacts in the business community."

Carson breathed a sigh of relief. Though Audra had told him she could bring a guest, he'd felt like a gate-crasher. Especially when Audra had run into some friends she hadn't seen in a while and he'd been left to mingle on his own. So far, other than Libby, he hadn't seen anyone he knew.

Carson let his gaze drift around the tastefully appointed room. "It's a lovely party. And the food is fabulous."

"How kind of you to say so." The tiny frown furrowing the older woman's brow eased. "I'm using a new caterer tonight and I have to admit I was a bit apprehensive. You know how it is, leaving the tried-and-true for something unknown."

"I can't comment on your previous caterers." Carson was careful to keep his voice casual and offhand. "But these appetizers are unique, not the same old crab puffs you've seen a thousand times before. And the desserts have been flying off the trays. I'm considering asking if the caterer would be interested in doing some specialty desserts for my restaurant."

"Hmm." Mrs. St. James gaze shifted to the guests milling around the dessert table. "Everyone does seem to be enjoying the food. It makes me glad I decided to give Peggy Summers a chance.''

''Summers?'' Carson couldn't hide his surprise.

''Yes, she's the owner of Elegant Affairs Catering,'' Mrs. St. James said. ''Do you know her?''

''I know her daughter.'' Even as he said the words, Carson wondered why Libby had told him her mother was a housekeeper but neglected to mention the woman also owned her own catering business. Of course, they hadn't done much talking the last few days. He'd been too busy with work to chat and she'd been strangely silent.

''Well, if her daughter is anything like her mother, I'm sure she's quite wonderful.''

''She is,'' Carson said. ''She's the best.''

''Are you two talking about me?'' After being gone for almost an hour, Audra seemed to appear out of nowhere. She slipped her hand through Carson's arm and brushed a kiss across his cheek.

Carson shifted, uncomfortable with Audra's sudden ''friendliness.''

Mrs. St. James's smile dimmed.

''We *have* been talking about you,'' Carson said diplomatically. ''And we've also been talking about the great food.''

''I'm sure it doesn't taste nearly as good as I do.'' An impish smile tipped Audra's lips. Then, suddenly, as if to illustrate, she rose on her tiptoes and this time kissed him full on the mouth.

She tasted like peppermint and her lips were warm and soft. But even if this would have been the time and place for such a display of affection, Carson wasn't even tempted to kiss her back.

Mrs. St. James shook her head disapprovingly. "I think someone needs to switch to mineral water and leave the champagne alone."

"I only had a few glasses." Audra shifted her gaze to Carson. "Besides, Carson likes it when I'm naughty. Don't you, Carson?"

He wasn't quite sure what she was talking about so he just smiled. His gaze lifted over her shoulder to the other side of the room where Libby now stood, replenishing a stack of plates on one of the dessert tables.

Though Libby's dress brushed her knees and the style was definitely not haute couture, there was something appealing in the simple look.

"Carson?"

He shifted his gaze back to the two women, realizing they were waiting for an answer.

But Carson still couldn't resist one last glance at Libby.

"Yes," he said finally. "Yes, I like it very much."

Chapter Ten

Carson wheeled his 4x4 into Audra's driveway and turned off the ignition. Though it had been a long day, it had been a productive one. He'd not only been able to meet Rand, the mayor's chief of staff, but they'd talked for almost an hour about the mayor's vision for the Santa Barbara business community.

In the end, it had been Rand who'd asked if Carson might be interested in serving on a new task force on business development. It couldn't have worked out more perfectly. And Carson knew he had Audra to thank.

His gaze shifted sideways to the blonde. She was a hard one to figure out. But he had to believe that the not-so-subtle messages she'd been sending him all evening were more a function of the champagne than any real interest in him.

"I want to thank you again for inviting me to the party," Carson said. "The contacts I made tonight were invaluable. I—"

"Does everything with you always have to be about business?" Audra tilted her head, a smile tipping her lips.

"Not always," he said finally. "But I specifically came with you tonight so you could introduce me around."

"Carson, someone needs to show you that there's more to life than P&L statements and business plans." Her voice turned low and husky. "You need to relax, live a little."

Carson had heard the sentiment a million times before. It wouldn't do any good to tell her all the time and effort it took to make a new business successful. Or the money it took to help support Becca and Seth. She wouldn't be interested and she wouldn't understand.

Audra had been born into a life of privilege. Granted, she worked hard as a marketing representative for her family's business, but Pacific Meats was a well-established company, not a new one fighting to survive in a tough market. And she had only herself to worry about. Still, he reminded himself that the fact that she wasn't facing an uphill struggle wasn't her fault, and the last thing he wanted to do was come across as condescending. He chose his words carefully.

"There *is* more to life than work," Carson admitted. "Unfortunately my responsibilities have to take priority in my life."

"How about for tonight?" She leaned forward and the sultry scent of her perfume filled his nostrils.

"Tonight?" Carson lifted a brow. "I'm not going to the restaurant tonight, if that's what you're asking."

"Good." Her lips curved up in a smile. "What about tomorrow?"

"Not until noon." Carson returned her smile, not sure why the sudden interest in his work schedule. "It's getting late. I'll walk you to the door."

He half expected her to protest—after all it was just a few steps to her house—but she waited patiently while he got out of the vehicle and rounded the front of the Jeep. After opening the passenger door he held out his hand and she stepped down with a long-legged grace that was as much a part of her as her diamond earrings.

Carson had to admit Audra looked especially lovely this evening. The shimmering jade fabric of her dress made her eyes look even greener and the style accentuated her soft curves. He couldn't help but notice how her hips swayed gently from side to side as they walked to the front door of her beachfront home. But while he could recognize and even appreciate such beauty, Carson didn't feel the slightest stirring of desire.

The porch light must have been motion sensitive because it clicked on as they approached. Though a kiss at the end of a date had become almost de rigueur, Carson wasn't even thinking about it when they reached the front step. After all, like he'd told her, tonight had been business, not social.

That's why he was caught off guard when Audra threw her arms around his neck and once again pressed her lips to his. Her mouth was soft and he could almost taste the champagne.

When the kiss ended, Carson took a step back and smiled. "Good night, Audra."

"What's the rush?" She leaned back against the door and studied him for a long moment. "Why don't you come in?"

Carson shook his head. "I have stuff to do in the morning. So, it's off to bed for me."

"Finally you and I are on the same wavelength." Audra gazed up at him through lowered lashes, her green eyes glittering like emeralds. "Would you think I was being too bold if I asked you to spend the night?"

Carson couldn't hide his surprise. "I thought neither one of us wanted that kind of relationship."

Audra laughed, a silvery tinkle of a laugh.

"I'm not talking about a relationship, silly." Her fingers walked up his arms. "I'm just talking about tonight. You. Me. Having fun. No ties. No expectations."

For one brief second Carson considered the offer. After all, Audra was a beautiful woman. But then he thought of Becca and remembered that one night of pleasure could change your entire life.

"Audra," he said softly, "I don't think that would be a good idea."

Her eyes widened and shock and disbelief skittered across her face. "You're saying no?"

Carson leaned forward and brushed a kiss across her cheek. "I'm saying good-night."

Before he could change his mind and do something they'd both regret, Carson turned on his heel and headed back to his vehicle.

As he slid behind the wheel, he glanced at the clock on the dash. Twelve-thirty. The restaurant wouldn't close for another half hour.

Though he had to be at church at eight, Carson turned the car in the direction of the Waterfront. Audra may not know him that well, but she was right about one thing—business did come first.

"I can't believe you made me do this." Libby shut the car door and followed Peggy up the steep sidewalk to the clapboard structure glimmering in the early-morning light.

Peggy chuckled. "You act as if I asked you to rob a bank."

"Getting up at seven on a Sunday may not be a

felony but it should be a crime.'' Libby swallowed a yawn.

Last night when Peggy had told Libby she'd pick her up shortly before eight for church, Libby had been so surprised at her assumption she hadn't known what to say. When she'd finally found her voice, it hadn't made a difference. Peggy had reminded her that she'd taken over Sierra's life and part of that life was attending Sunday services.

''You'll enjoy Pastor Reimnitz's sermons,'' Peggy said, climbing the steps. ''He does a great job of taking today's issues and relating them to the Bible.''

Reserving judgment, Libby just smiled and followed Peggy into the church. It had been years since she'd walked into a house of worship other than for a wedding or funeral. And her last recollection of a regular service hadn't been all that pleasant. She doubted this morning would be any different.

But halfway through the sermon, Libby realized that Peggy was right. The minister was a good speaker and she found the topic of living your faith interesting, especially in light of her recent discussion with Carson.

The service went quickly and before she knew it, they were singing the closing hymn.

''There, see.'' As they left the church, Peggy looped her arm around Libby's shoulders and gave her a quick hug. ''That wasn't so bad, was it?''

Libby smiled sheepishly. ''It was okay.''

"Libby."

A familiar male voice sounded above the din of the crowd exiting the church.

Libby whirled.

Carson stood at the top of the church steps. He lifted one hand in greeting and then began weaving his way through the crowd toward her.

"Who's that?" Peggy's appreciative gaze lingered on Carson's lean form.

"Carson Davies," Libby said, never taking her gaze from him.

Peggy's eyes widened. "That's your boss?"

Libby nodded.

"He's gorgeous." Peggy's voice held a hint of awe.

Libby understood. She'd felt that same way when she'd first seen the man.

Today, instead of khakis and a polo shirt he wore his Sunday best: a dark blue suit, crisp white shirt and a conservatively striped tie. His hair glistened like a golden halo in the bright California sun.

Libby glanced down at her sleeveless dress. A yellow linen sheath had replaced last night's uniform, and instead of the clunky black oxfords, strappy sandals of pale lemon graced her perfectly pedicured feet.

She barely had time to smooth a wrinkle from her skirt before Carson broke through the masses and moved to her side.

"I know you said you went to this church," Carson said, gazing at her with an appreciative smile, "but with so many services I wasn't sure I'd run into you or not."

Libby lifted a brow and tried hard not to let her utter delight at seeing him show. "What are you doing here?"

"I spoke to a couple of the early-morning Bible study groups about the food bank," he said.

Libby wondered if his words would make sense if she'd had her coffee. "I'm afraid you've lost me. What do cans of green beans and boxes of corn bread have to do with Bible study?"

"The groups are currently focusing on how to live your faith and minister to others. So Pastor R. asked me to stop by and speak." Carson smiled and turned to Peggy. He extended his hand. "I don't believe we've met. I'm Carson Davies. Libby and I work together."

"Peggy Summers." The older woman took his hand, smiling almost coquettishly. "Libby and I—"

"Are mother and daughter." Libby finished the sentence for her. She knew it was impolite to interrupt, but for a second she'd sworn that Peggy had been so taken by Carson's charm that she'd been about to forget her role in this whole charade. "She's my mother."

"It's a pleasure to meet you, Mrs. Summers." Carson's gaze slid from Peggy to Libby and she could see him trying to find a resemblance between the two, but quickly giving up. "Well, I'd better get going. I just wanted to say hello."

"Libby and I were going to grab some brunch downtown," Peggy said. "Would you like to join us?"

Libby shot Peggy a warning gaze, but Peggy's gaze never wavered from Carson's face.

Carson hesitated. "I wouldn't want to intrude...."

Peggy waved a dismissive hand. "You wouldn't be intruding at all. We'd love to have you join us. Wouldn't we, Libby?"

Carson's gaze shifted to Libby and she offered him a polite smile. Even though she'd like to spend time with Carson, she couldn't help but worry that in a casual setting Peggy might say too much.

"It would be nice." Libby kept any encouragement from her voice, hoping Carson would pick up on her reticence and decline the invitation. "Of course, we'll understand if you're too busy...."

"I think I can spare an hour or so," he said, flashing that charming smile that always made Libby's heart do flip-flops. "I've been hoping to talk to your mother about her catering business and this will give me that chance."

Though Libby hadn't been sure it was a good idea for him to join them, she couldn't help but be slightly miffed that the reason he'd said yes didn't have a single thing to do with her.

* * *

Libby watched Peggy walk out the front door of the café, her step jaunty and a tiny smile on her cinnamon-colored lips. Once they'd been seated, Peggy had *unexpectedly* remembered a meeting with a prospective catering client. She'd made her exit after securing Carson's promise to drop Libby off at home.

"We don't need to eat," Libby said, closing her menu and setting it aside. She felt as if Peggy had foisted her on Carson. After all, he'd only come along so that he could talk to Peggy about her catering business. Now the woman had taken off and left before they'd even started that discussion. "I know you're in a hurry."

He smiled and that cute little dimple in his left cheek flashed. "Libby Summers, if I didn't know better, I'd think you were trying to get rid of me."

"Believe me, if I wanted to get rid of you, you'd know it," Libby said with an impish smile.

Carson laughed and opened his menu. The conversation flowed easily and naturally. It seemed like only minutes after they'd ordered that the waiter arrived with their food.

Libby took a bite of her ham-and-cheese quiche and silently thanked Peggy for making her go to church this morning. If she hadn't gone, she wouldn't have seen Carson. And she wouldn't be enjoying this wonderful lunch with him now.

"There's one thing that I can't figure out." Carson took a bite of his sandwich and chewed thoughtfully. "Why isn't someone as pretty as you married?"

Libby inhaled sharply and almost choked on a piece of ham. In the last couple of years Libby had started hearing that question or variations of it with increasing frequency. But it was Carson tossing it out in the middle of a conversation about the restaurant industry that had caught her off guard.

For most men, laughter was enough of an answer, but from Carson's expectant gaze she knew he expected more. "I've never found a man I could trust. Or one who I could love who loved me back. How about you?"

His gaze grew thoughtful but, like her, he didn't seem surprised by the question. He'd likely been put on the spot more than once, too. After all, any man or woman who reached their mid-twenties without a ring on their finger was fair game.

"There has always been so much I've wanted to accomplish," Carson said finally. "I've never given myself the time, or the permission, to fall in love."

"What about your date the other night?" Libby toyed with her fork. "Are you two serious?"

Carson shook his head. "Audra is a nice woman. But we're only friends, business associates really."

"You're not romantically involved?" Libby took another bite of quiche, pleased she could sound so offhand when her heart was pounding so loud she could barely hear herself speak.

"Not at all," Carson said. "Like I said, I don't have much free time, and even if I did, I don't think Audra and I are well suited. What about you? Anyone special in your life?"

Libby paused. The other night she'd told him about Stephen. Could he have already forgotten?

"Nobody right now," she said. "To tell you the truth, that's fine with me. I mean, it would be nice to have someone to go to places with or hang out with when I have some free time, but right now school is my priority."

It wasn't entirely true, but it had enough elements of truth to be reasonably accurate.

"I feel the same way." Carson leaned forward, resting his arms on the table. "I'd like to have someone to take to different events, but it seems like after a few dates women start expecting more, and I don't have more to give."

His gaze turned cloudy and Libby couldn't help but wonder if that's what had really happened between him and Audra. Audra certainly wouldn't be the first woman who wanted more than a man was prepared to give. Libby felt almost sorry for the beautiful blonde. She'd been in that position herself way too many times.

"Believe me," Libby said. "I understand completely."

Carson stared at her for a long moment.

Libby shifted uncomfortably under his intense gaze.

"I may have a solution," Carson said. "One that could solve both of our problems."

The look in his eye was disturbing and exciting at the same time. "What do you mean?"

"I could be your date when you need one," he said. "You could do the same for me."

Libby's heart took a flying leap in her chest. She was definitely in the mood for summer fun. Still, Libby wasn't sure the arrangement would work.

"With our schedules being so hectic, we wouldn't be that available for each other," she said.

"True." Carson nodded his agreement. "But that's something that would be understood up front. We could ask each other about a specific event and if it works, it works. If the time works, it works. If it doesn't, we're no worse off than we are now."

Libby considered his words. "What if I just wanted someone to hang out with?"

"Same thing," he said. "If the timing works, great. If not, no big deal."

"What if we found someone we really liked?" she said, trying to think of every eventuality. "What then?"

"Same thing," he repeated. "We could walk away with no—"

"Recriminations," she said with a smile.

"Exactly." Carson picked up his sandwich and gazed at her over the country roll stuffed with prime rib. "What do you think?"

Libby paused. She was so incredibly tempted to throw caution to the winds and just say yes. Carson would certainly be a pleasant distraction from the drudgery of work and she would know at the onset that he didn't want anything more from her than companionship. So, hopefully she could keep her heart out of the equation. That left only one minor issue to resolve.

"What about kissing?" she asked. "Would we kiss?"

Carson's gaze lowered and her lips started to tingle.

"I don't see why not." He offered her an easy smile. "That is, I'd be agreeable if you wanted to add that to our arrangement."

"I can't imagine spending so much time together and not kissing," Libby said in as casual of a tone as she could muster.

His smile widened. "I agree completely."

Chapter Eleven

I can't imagine spending so much time together and not kissing.

Carson groaned and placed his arm around his nephew's shoulder. He leaned back in the sofa and tried to focus on the Disney video. But his mind kept returning to his lunchtime conversation with Libby. He still couldn't believe he'd agreed with that statement.

His gaze shifted sideways to the young woman sitting in a nearby chair. She hummed as she stitched the final finishing touches on a shirt she'd made for the boy at his side. Becca's shoulder-length brown hair was pulled back in a loose ponytail and her jean shorts and T-shirt were more comfortable than fashionable. Despite having a child, her figure was as trim as before her pregnancy and her face still held a youthful innocence.

He'd spent a lot of time with Becca these past two years and not once had the thought of kissing her even crossed his mind. Though, he had to admit there were times the look in her eye made him wonder if it had crossed hers. But then he'd remind himself that it was Cole she was seeing when she looked at him with such intense longing.

The first time Cole had brought Becca home to meet his family, she'd been shocked to find out her boyfriend was an identical twin. Apparently Cole had told her that he had two brothers, but had left out the fact that he and Carson were exact replicas.

Maybe it was because Cole had been struggling to forge his own identity, to find his own way. Carson knew who he was and why he was on the earth while Cole was questioning everything, including the faith that had been a part of his life since childhood.

They hadn't expected to see Cole that Christmas. He'd called earlier in the week and said he wouldn't be able to make it. So they were surprised when he not only showed up, but brought a girl.

Though Becca was younger than Cole by almost four years, the two of them had seemed well suited. Even Connor, the youngest of the three brothers and normally oblivious to such things, had commented on how happy Cole had been that Christmas. That's why they'd been surprised when Cole had decided after graduation to go ahead with earlier plans to go to Africa with a group of activists.

Becca had been distraught and Cole had made Carson promise to look after her if anything happened to him. Although Carson had agreed, at the time he couldn't imagine anything happening to his compassionate, idealistic, older-by-two-minutes brother.

But it seemed Cole had reason to be concerned. Two weeks after his arrival in the Congo, the State Department advised them that Cole had been killed in a civil uprising. The whole family had been devastated at the news. Later their sadness was tempered with bittersweet joy when Becca discovered she was pregnant with Cole's baby.

Although Becca had no family and very little money, she'd been determined to continue the pregnancy and keep the baby. They'd supported her decision and had accepted her into their family.

But with his mother already working two jobs to help his youngest brother pay for college, the burden had fallen on Carson to fill the void left by Cole's absence. Carson willingly took on the role of surrogate father. He and Cole had grown up without a father and they'd promised each other that no child of theirs would grow up without a man in their life.

Seth had been a sickly baby, with one illness after another. And the boy's problems made it difficult for Becca to do anything but take care of him and finish her education.

Carson had worked harder and longer to bring in extra money for the additional expenses. Supporting a woman and a child at this stage in his life hadn't been in Carson's plans, but he decided it must have been in God's plans.

Seth giggled at the silly animal on the screen and Carson's gaze settled lovingly on the little towheaded boy. Seth was the spitting image of his father at that age and smart as a whip. Unfortunately, his health problems had continued and he'd recently been diagnosed with asthma. Though the doctors had assured them with proper medication Seth should be able to avoid any future trips to the emergency room, Becca had grown even more protective of her son.

Becca lifted her gaze from her sewing and smiled at Seth before shifting her gaze to Carson. "Your mother tells me you're dating someone new?"

Carson paused, not sure who his mother could have meant. He hadn't had what he'd call a real date in months.

"Audra?" Becca's brows furrowed. "I think that's the name she mentioned."

"Audra and I went out a couple of times," Carson said. "But it was more a business kind of thing than anything romantic."

"You need to be more social, Carson." Becca gave a little laugh. "What am I saying? *I* need to be more social."

Carson smiled, knowing it was true. Becca had had

a birthday just last week and had ended up spending it at the emergency room with Seth.

"I've got an idea," Becca said. "I was talking to your mom today and she said there's going to be a street dance at the San Rafael festival this year. She offered to watch Seth. I told her that wasn't necessary but she insisted. Maybe we could go together? That way we'll both be more social and your mother will be happy."

Carson stifled a groan. He liked Becca, liked her a lot in fact. But like a sister, not like a girlfriend.

"Getting a group together does sound like fun," Carson said, deliberately misunderstanding her words. "I'll ask at work and see how many I can round up to join us."

"The more the merrier." A hint of pink touched Becca's cheeks and he knew she'd seen through his ruse but had decided not to call him on it.

It made Carson feel bad, but he couldn't date her. He could be a father to Seth and a friend of Becca. But as long as Becca and Cole were linked in his mind, that's where it had to stop. His mother might think a match between the two of them made perfect sense, but a tiny part of Carson still held out hope that his brother hadn't died. And as long as Carson held this hope, he couldn't be anything more to Becca, no matter how much sense everyone thought it made.

* * *

It was nearly eleven before Carson pulled into Santa Barbara. All the way home he could only think of Libby.

If he had her address in his Palm Pilot, he'd be half tempted to swing by her house and see if the light was on. After all, friends often stopped by to say hello even at such late hours.

If she was still up, he could try to see if she'd be interested in a cup of coffee or better yet, a walk on the beach.

They could take a blanket and spread it out on the sand, then lie back and study the stars. Because that's what friends do when they hang out. They share information about constellations and meteor showers. They discuss their plans for the upcoming week. And sometimes, when the conversation falters, they even kiss.

But Carson didn't have her address.

Or her phone number.

And it was too late to drive back to the Waterfront and get that information.

Disappointment flowed through him and he was so deep into his thoughts that he barely noticed a car parked on the street in front of his town house.

But when he pulled into the drive, a feminine form stepped out from the shadows and caught his eye.

Carson's heart picked up speed.

Though it was slightly overcast, the night had suddenly turned bright.

A friend had come to visit.

Chapter Twelve

Carson wheeled the Jeep into the carport and screeched to a stop. He'd barely shut off the engine before he flung open the door and hopped out, his heart picking up speed.

It was crazy that he and Libby were already on the same wavelength. Here, he'd just been thinking of her and suddenly there she was, waiting for him.

He quickened his step, wondering if the reason she'd stayed by the front door rather than coming to immediately greet him was because of embarrassment. Even though they'd talked about it being okay just to stop by, it couldn't have been easy for her to make the first move. Carson smiled. He'd make sure she felt properly welcomed.

But the minute Carson rounded the corner, he stopped short. Disappointment replaced his boyish eagerness and his smile vanished. "Audra. What are you doing here?"

The leggy blonde shifted uncomfortably from one foot to another and her artificially bright smile faded at the shock in his voice. But she lifted her chin and stared at him without a hint of apology in her gaze. "I realize it's late. Unfortunately what I have to say can't wait."

Carson stared at the beautiful blonde and rubbed a weary hand across his face. Suddenly he was very tired. He wished he could ask her to come back at a more reasonable hour but his mother had raised him to be a gentleman. "Shall we talk inside?"

He unlocked the dead bolt and pushed the door open. Turning on the light, Carson stepped aside to let her enter.

"Cute place," Audra said with a decided lack of enthusiasm.

Personally Carson thought his mother and Becca had done a fabulous job making the modest quarters look nice and homey. But he knew it paled in comparison to Audra's home in Hope Ranch.

The thought didn't bother Carson in the least.

"Have a seat." Carson waved a hand toward the sofa. "Can I get you something to drink?"

"This isn't really a social call." Audra moved across the room and took a seat in a rattan chair.

"Don't tell me you want to talk business at this hour?" Carson took a seat on the couch she'd spurned and smiled. "And you accuse me of being driven."

To his surprise, Audra didn't even crack a smile at the teasing. Instead, she leaned forward, her expression intense and utterly serious.

"I need you to do something for me," she said. "It's really important."

For the first time Carson noticed the tiny lines furrowing her brow and the tightness of the hands folded in her lap.

"What's the matter, Audra?" Concern replaced his teasing grin.

Audra met his gaze. "When I invited you to come inside and spend the night I didn't mean it."

Carson stared.

A flush of pink touched her cheeks.

"I mean I meant it at the time." The words tumbled out one after the other, a slight tremble underscoring them. "But I think it was that blasted champagne punch talking. I'm not usually so forward or so undiscriminating."

Carson sat back in his chair and burst into laughter. "If you'd wanted to insult me you could have done it anytime. You didn't have to make a special trip."

Audra brushed back a stray strand of hair and smiled as if she'd just now realized what she'd said. "I just meant we hadn't known each other that long. I'm not saying there's anything wrong with you."

"Whew." Carson pretended to wipe sweat from his brow. "That's a relief."

Audra leaned back in her chair and studied him for a moment, the smile still hovering on the corners of her lips. "In fact, you're fairly cute. If you like that surfer look, that is. Which I don't."

Carson had to laugh again. "Okay, enough already. Just tell me what you want from me."

"You know that Brian and I are good friends." Audra shifted her gaze over Carson's shoulder and the pink that dusted her cheeks deepened to a dark rose. "What you don't know is that I've been in love with him for years."

Carson hesitated, stunned by the unexpected revelation. He'd known Brian considered Audra to be one of his best friends, but Carson had never suspected anything more. "I didn't even know you two were dating."

"We haven't. I mean we aren't." Audra raised her hand when Carson started to speak. "Just to clarify, I'm the one interested, not him."

"And this has what to do with me?" Carson shifted in his chair.

"I need a favor." Audra met his gaze head-on. "Don't tell Brian I acted so foolishly the other night."

"I never even considered saying anything to Brian," Carson said immediately, not even needing to think about his answer.

Audra's gaze searched his. "Really?"

"You have my word." Carson smiled, glad her request could be fulfilled so easily. "My lips are sealed."

The tension visibly left Audra's shoulders and she flashed a relieved smile as she rose to her feet. "Thanks, Carson. I owe you."

Carson followed her lead and stood. "You don't owe me anything."

He looped an arm companionably around Audra's shoulders and they walked to her car. He waited until she'd driven out of sight before he returned to the house.

Once inside, he pulled the door firmly shut, wishing he didn't have to worry about extraneous women in his life.

He didn't want to think about Becca and her need for a new man in her life or Audra and her unrequited love for his business partner. There was only one woman on his mind tonight, only one woman he wanted to think about, only one woman he wanted: his new best friend, Libby Summers.

Libby walked through the door of the Sunrise Coffee Company at a quarter to eight. Despite the early-morning hour she felt strangely refreshed. Maybe it was because she'd had such a great night. She'd spent most of the evening at Peggy's house. Sierra and Maddie had been there and they'd made it a "girl's night.'' They'd snacked on popcorn and Peggy's homemade brownies and watched a marathon of G-rated movies.

Maddie had been at her most adorable. When she wrapped her little arms around Libby's neck and laid her head on Libby's chest, Libby had found herself wondering what it would be like to have a daughter of her own. But she'd shoved the crazy thought aside, reminding herself that children weren't even on her radar screen. She was still kissing frogs....

Libby's lips lifted in a smile. After yesterday's conversation with Carson, waiting for today had been pure torture. She'd slept soundly, and for the first time she'd been out of bed before the alarm had even sounded.

But on her drive to work the yawns had begun and she'd had to make a detour for a scone and a cup of her favorite brew.

Libby smiled a thanks to the older gentleman who'd held the door open for her and headed straight for the bakery case. Though there were three people ahead of her and only one scone, Libby wasn't worried. She had a feeling the biscuit would still be there when it was her turn. It just seemed like that kind of day.

Sure enough, the two men in line only ordered drinks and the teen standing directly in front of her didn't even give the scone a second glance.

Libby placed her order and scrounged in her

pocket for some spare change. She was continually amazed at how quickly Sierra's paycheck disappeared. But Libby wasn't about to let money worries taint her mood. She gave the guy behind the counter a handful of coins and moved to the side, eagerly anticipating the taste of the snickerdoodle coffee and scone. To still the thought that she was now completely out of money until Friday, she hummed along to the familiar tune playing overhead.

"We're going to have to stop meeting like this."

Libby whirled, her lips curving up in a broad welcoming smile. "Carson. What are you doing here?"

He gestured to several men heading out the door. "I had a meeting. How about you?"

Libby took the coffee from the woman behind the counter and held up the scone. "It's my lucky day."

"Funny." He tilted his head and smiled lazily. "That was exactly my thought when I saw you walk through that door."

A shiver traveled up Libby's spine. She couldn't believe it. The day just kept getting better and better. "I was planning to drink this in the car, but it would certainly be nice to sit and relax for a few minutes."

Carson studied Libby for an extra beat before he smiled. She wasn't fooling him. He knew what this sit-and-relax stuff was all about. It was Monday and Libby was no more eager to jump into work mode than he was. He mentally reviewed his morning schedule and decided there was nothing on his desk that couldn't wait a few minutes. "Sounds good to me."

He followed Libby to an empty table by the window, pulling out her chair while admiring the long slender lines of her legs.

"How was your evening?" Libby asked, taking a sip of her coffee and nibbling on the scone.

Carson leaned back in his chair and lifted one shoulder in a noncommittal shrug. "I went to San Rafael."

For a second, confusion clouded Libby's brow, but then she nodded. "That's right. You told me you were from north of here."

She broke off a piece of scone. "Does your mother still live there?"

Carson nodded. "She can't imagine living anywhere else."

"What about your brothers?" Libby took another sip of coffee.

Carson shook his head, a stabbing pain slicing his heart the way it always did when he thought of Cole. "My younger brother, Connor, is away at college." He swallowed hard. "My other brother, Cole, left for Africa a couple of years ago. He was there for humanitarian purposes but he got caught in the middle of a political coup."

Libby set her cup on the table and her expression grew serious. "What happened to him?"

Carson cleared his throat. "Actually the authorities say he was killed. But his body was never found."

Her eyes widened. "He died?"

"I don't know. That's what the government says." Carson briefly shifted his gaze out the window, remembering the call. "But Cole and I have always been close. I can't help but think if he were dead I'd know it."

"That has to be hard." Libby reached across the table and gave his hand a squeeze.

"It is hard." His heart tightened in his chest. "You lost your father. You know what it is to lose someone you love."

"I do know what it's like…to have someone you love so much no longer be in your life." A melancholy look filled her eyes and she paused for the longest time. "Do you ever wonder why such things happen? Why a loving God would even allow such things to happen?"

Her questions were ones he'd struggled with, questions he still struggled with when memories of Cole surfaced and the pain flared.

"Even though everything in my life hasn't always gone the way I would have liked," Carson said finally, "I've never questioned God's love. God has been the one constant in my life. The One I could always depend on."

Libby leaned forward in her chair, her long slender

fingers curved around the ceramic mug. "But losing your father—"

"It was hard, but some good did come of it." Carson remembered back. "Until Dad died we'd never been much of a churchgoing family. But the congregation down the block was wonderfully supportive during that time and the whole experience strengthened our faith. I don't know if that would have happened otherwise."

"What about your brother?" Libby asked. "What good came of that?"

He thought for a long moment. "I took Cole for granted. I assumed he'd always be around. His absence has taught me that if you care about someone you need to let them know. You may not have another chance."

Carson knew if he hadn't been able to lay his troubles at the foot of the cross, he never would have survived the difficult times in his life. He started to say just that when he realized that not only had he been dominating the conversation, he was beginning to sound more than a little preachy.

"How about a walk?" Carson said, deliberately shifting focus. "It's a beautiful morning."

"Rejoice in the day the Lord has made?" Libby said with a smile.

"Exactly." Carson rose to his feet and held out his hand.

Libby hesitated. "What about work?"

He shot her a conspiratorial wink. "If you don't tell the boss, I won't."

She laughed and took his hand. "Does it matter where we go?"

Carson smiled and shook his head, his eyes drawn to her lips. Actually it didn't matter. Not at all.

Chapter Thirteen

Carson's hand was warm and Libby liked the feel of his skin against hers. Although she had never been into public displays of affection, this was different. They weren't lovers groping each other, they were merely friends holding hands and enjoying a little time together.

They ambled down the sidewalk, the early-morning sun already hot and bright. With no destination in mind, they walked aimlessly, stopping only occasionally to glance in shop windows.

Libby made a conscious effort to keep the conversation light and easy. She regretted letting their earlier discussion get out of hand. She'd practically interrogated the poor guy, and goodness knows she wouldn't have wanted someone to do that to her. But she'd been curious about his family. And she'd wanted to know what made him tick. Still, his words about faith and God made her uncomfortable. It was the same feeling she got when Sierra talked about having a personal relationship with God.

Both of them seemed convinced that the Almighty loved everyone. Libby didn't agree. Carson and Sierra and others worthy of such unconditional love were caring souls who would be impossible not to love.

They weren't like her. They would never deliberately refuse to return their mother's phone calls just because they knew the calls would hurt her. They would never say cruel things to people just because they were angry. And they certainly would never resent spending a couple hours a week in worship just because they'd wanted to sleep late.

No, Libby felt certain that God, like everyone else, would find a person with such faults difficult to love.

It was a fact of life and Libby didn't dwell on the thought. The air was soft against her cheek, the sun was shining and the handsome man next to her made her pulse race just by glancing her way. It was too pleasant a day to ruin with pointless introspection.

They continued to walk and soon left downtown behind, moving into the residential area. The farther they walked, the more impressive the homes were.

Built in the late 1800s, the grounds of these Victorians were spacious blankets of green dotted with

large trees and a seemingly endless supply of bloom-
ing flowers.

They weren't far now from Libby's home. In fact,
if they walked much farther, they'd pass her front
door. But at the end of the next block Carson unexpectedly slowed his steps and stopped. He tipped his
head back and gazed at the impressive home that sat
back from the street, its red-tiled roof barely visible
through the break in the hedge.

"I've always wanted to live in this neighbor-
hood." Carson's appreciative gaze lingered on the
painted scrollwork beneath the uppermost eave. He
gave a little shrug. "Maybe someday."

"If you had a rich wife, she could make that dream
come true right now," Libby said in a light tone. The
moment the words left her mouth Libby wondered if
she was forever destined to judge all men based on
her father's low standards.

Carson just laughed. "You sound like Brian."

"I'm not sure that's a compliment," Libby said
with a teasing smile, noticing he didn't dispute her
words.

"I didn't intend it to be." Carson grinned. He
moved close to the slight opening in the tall foliage
surrounding the property's perimeter. "Doesn't that
look like it could be part of a maze?"

Libby didn't even have to look where he pointed.
Her mother was good friends with Mary, the woman
who owned the home. There was indeed a maze in

the yard, one that had fascinated Libby ever since she'd been ten years old and had gotten lost in it.

"C'mon." Libby tugged on his hand. "Let me show you something."

Carson was one step behind her as they rounded the corner of the property. He followed without protest when she stepped on the grass and then into a barely perceptible opening between two large bushes. But when she started to squeeze through, Carson laid a restraining hand on her arm.

"I don't think we should," he said. "We'll be trespassing."

"I know the woman," Libby said. "If she were in town, we could ask her. But, trust me, she won't care."

Still, Carson hesitated. For a second she wondered how she could be so attracted to someone who didn't seem to have a risk-taking bone in his body, but then she decided that was probably part of his appeal. After all, didn't they say opposites attract?

"It's the truth," Libby said. "Now, are you coming with me? Or am I going to have to call you…Chicken Man?"

The words were from her childhood, the taunting friends gave each other to force compliance. She added a few clucking noises and he smiled, shaking his head.

"Lead the way," he said. "I just hope it's worth the risk."

* * *

Halfway through the maze, Libby and Carson paused to rest on a wooden bench against the hedge wall. With the sun beating down overhead and very little air circulating, the temperature soared within the five-foot-wide path.

Carson didn't seem to notice the heat. He gazed admiringly at the perfectly manicured foliage rising almost eight feet into the air. "I have to admit that this was worth it."

Libby shot him a smug smile and leaned back. "Aren't you glad you weren't a—"

She paused and let loose with a couple of clucks. She had to do it. It had simply been too long since she'd had the opportunity to show off her skill. When she'd been little, Sierra had been a master at oinking like a pig, while Libby's specialty had been the chicken.

Carson groaned. "That's the worst chicken imitation I've ever heard."

Libby stared in disbelief. Her clucks were second to none. She opened her mouth to give him another sample of her skill, but before the sound could pass her lips, Carson leaned close and pressed his hand briefly against her mouth. "Not one more squawk. Understand?"

He was only inches away, so close that Libby could see the gold flecks in his blue eyes and smell the spicy scent of his cologne. Libby's breath caught in her throat. The childishness was forgotten. All she could think of was how beautiful he was, how perfect. How overwhelmingly male in every way.

They were face-to-face, his mouth now only a kiss away. She stared deep into his eyes and forced herself to breathe.

"I'm not sure I trust you to keep quiet." His dark blue gaze locked with hers and for a second she swore he could see her innermost thoughts. He took in the rest of her features slowly, then finally came to rest on her mouth. "Maybe I should find a better way to seal those lips."

"Maybe you should," Libby said, her voice low and husky with the awareness that he had indeed managed to read her mind. Her breathing deepened in anticipation.

Carson's hand traveled up her arm to her shoulder, then his fingers slipped through the hair at the nape of her neck.

Her throat grew dry and she swallowed hard.

Using his other hand to push her hair back from her face, Carson bent down and gently covered her mouth with his.

His lips were warm and soft, the scent of him musky and all male. Carson lifted his head and met her gaze, his dark, intense look telling her how much this moment meant to him, too.

"Not to complain, but I don't know if that did the trick." Though Libby's heart beat hard and fast, she managed to keep her voice steady. "Once aroused, the urge to cluck can be very strong, very difficult to suppress."

Carson might be a straight arrow, but he was a man, and a smart one at that. Without her needing to utter another word, he leaned over and kissed her again, longer this time, letting his mouth linger. It was just as sweet, though, just as gentle.

"Still have that urge?" A lazy smile hitched up the corner of his mouth.

A decidedly wicked tingle traveled up her spine. "Maybe we should do it again just to be sure."

Carson laughed and pulled her into his arms. "Great idea."

He lowered his head, crushed his lips to hers and swallowed her gasp of surprise. It took her only a second to realize that this was nothing like the sweet, gentle kisses they'd just shared.

This time as he kissed her, the world disappeared in a whirl of unexpected sensations. Her fingers curled into his shoulders, and she pulled him close. Dazed and breathing hard, she suddenly pulled back.

There was shock in Carson's eyes. "Libby, I'm—"

"I'm cured," she interrupted, trying to get a handle on the dizzying waves of heat and cold racking her body.

"Cured?" Carson said, still looking dazed.

Though her breath came in breathless puffs, Libby forced a smile. ''I don't feel the slightest urge to cluck.''

It was close to ten by the time they arrived at the restaurant. The employees werc busy getting ready for the lunch crowd and nobody seemed to notice they were late.

Carson pulled into the Waterfront's parking area right behind her. But when he walked through the front door, he headed straight to the dining room to confer with the new wait staff manager while Libby went upstairs to the office and began entering figures into the computer.

The mindless task suited her. Her brain was too filled with Carson's kisses to allow her to focus on anything that took any real thought. They'd had a wonderful morning together. In fact, it had been a long time since she'd had so much fun.

It was probably because she and Carson had set the ground rules from the beginning. They were friends, nothing more. And with friends you could do crazy things, such as squawk like a chicken or sneak through a fence or even kiss like a lovestruck teenager.

She remembered Stephen's insistence on maintaining propriety at all costs. Libby could only imagine the horrified look on Stephen's face if he'd heard her chicken noise. Her lips curved upward.

''Penny for your thoughts.'' Carson's hands closed around her shoulders.

Though she hadn't heard him come in, Libby wasn't surprised he couldn't stay away. It had taken all of her willpower to go her separate way when they'd hit the front door. She swiveled in the desk chair, smiled a welcome and tipped her face up to his. ''I was thinking about making those chicken noises.''

She hadn't said it because she wanted to weasel another kiss out of him, truly she hadn't. Still, when a spark flashed in his eyes and his gaze lowered to her mouth, she knew that was exactly the message he'd gotten.

But as he pulled her to her feet and his mouth closed over hers, Libby decided that sometimes miscommunication could be the best kind of communication.

Chapter Fourteen

Carson hadn't planned on kissing Libby again, not so soon and especially not at work. If he'd given it any thought, he would have talked himself out of it. He would have reminded himself of all the good, solid reasons why he shouldn't kiss her. But there she was, her mouth all soft and warm and inviting.

It was just a kiss, he thought dimly, delving his fingers through the warm, silky mass at the nape of her neck. His thumbs grazed the soft skin beneath her jaw as he angled his mouth to deepen the kiss. She tasted like peppermint, her mouth startled under his. Then she leaned into the kiss.

"No wonder you spend so much time at the office."

The words sounded far away, like the irritating buzz of a mosquito. While Carson was content to ignore the interruption, Libby pulled back with a re-gretful sigh.

Carson turned and his irritation soared when he encountered the smirking face of his business partner staring back at him from the doorway.

He'd never liked being surprised and he didn't like it now. And apparently neither did Libby. She started to step back, to put some distance between them, but he took her hand and kept her near his side. They weren't teenagers caught in a porch light's harsh glare and he wasn't going to act as if they'd done something wrong.

"I thought our meeting wasn't until eleven," Carson said, staring his partner straight in the eye.

"It *is* eleven," Brian said, feigning an innocent expression. "But if you want to continue with your, er, current business discussion, that's all right with me. I'll just sit and read a magazine or something."

Brian sauntered across the room, that knowing smirk still on his face, and took a seat in the chair against the wall.

Carson gritted his teeth. When he got his friend alone he was going to tell him just how much he didn't appreciate the interruption. But, judging from the grin on Brian's face, the man already knew.

"I promised the front staff I'd bring them some extra menus." Libby pulled her hand from Carson's grasp, flashed him a brilliant smile and scooped up a stack of menus from the corner of the desk. "I'll just take these down and see if they need any help."

The color was high in her cheeks, but other than that there were no signs that they'd been doing anything but having a meeting. If Brian hadn't barged in without knocking, that's what they could have claimed.

Carson admired her composure and he forced the same businesslike tone into his voice. "I have a lunch meeting at noon. How about we get together around one-thirty and I'll give you a quick orientation to the food donation program?"

"Sounds perfect." Libby smiled, then turned to his partner. "Nice to see you again, Brian."

Brian lifted a hand in a half salute, a lazy smile tipping his lips.

"You sly dog," Brian said, the moment the door closed. "When did your business relationship with the lovely Ms. Summers get so personal? Last time we talked you insisted she was just an employee."

"Cut it out, Brian." Carson took a seat behind the desk. He kept his tone deliberately curt, knowing if he gave his partner even the slightest indication the topic was open for discussion, he was sunk. "Libby and I are friends. Nothing more."

"Friends, eh?" A wicked gleam shone in Brian's eyes. "Personally I don't believe anyone can have too many friends, especially not of the luscious Libby variety. Do you think she could be my friend, too?"

"No," Carson said. "I don't."

The thought of Brian even touching Libby, much less kissing her, raised Carson's blood pressure to the boiling point. He tried hard not to let his anger show, knowing it would only give his friend more ammunition.

"If you're going to say she hates me," Brian said, "don't bother. You tried that old trick before. But ole Bri isn't stupid. He knows when you're foolin' him."

"You don't know anything." Carson ignored the exaggerated cornpone accent and picked up a report from his desk, pretending to study it.

"I know you've got it bad for your new employee," Brian said. "Just take a little advice from someone who knows—be careful."

"I can't believe it." Carson dropped the report to his desk. "*You* giving *me* advice on relationships."

"I'm serious," Brian said. "Libby is lovely, but she's also your employee."

"We're just friends," Carson said, his voice rising despite his best efforts to control it. "Why can't you understand that?"

"Because I'm not blind," Brian said with a wink. "I saw how you kissed her. And…the way she kissed you back."

It had been the most wonderful month of her life, Libby decided, smiling to herself as she hurried upstairs to the office. Not only had her new job coordinating the donations of food to the shelters been incredibly rewarding, the way her co-workers at the Waterfront had accepted her warmed her heart. For the first time Libby had proof that her ability to make friends wasn't irrevocably tied to her financial or social status. And though she hadn't gotten used to the lack of money, being poor had given her a new perspective.

The door to Carson's office was slightly ajar and the sound of music filtered into the hall. Anticipation coursed up Libby's spine. When she hadn't seen Carson at the coffee shop this morning, she'd worried that he might be out of town. Now it looked as if she'd worried for nothing.

Libby eased the door open and stood there for a moment. Carson sat at the desk with his back to her, his gaze focused on the computer screen. The morning light shone through the window and cast a halo of light on his golden hair.

Libby curbed a sudden urge to cross the room and rake her fingers through those silky strands. It was one of her favorite things to do while he was kissing her. Libby loved seeing his hair spiked out in all directions, making him look as though he'd just gotten out of bed. She loved the fresh scent of his shampoo against her face. But most of all, she loved him.

Her heart stilled for half a beat. Though the realization should have surprised her, somehow it didn't. Maybe because she'd suspected it for some time now.

When she wasn't with him, she missed him. It took only one smile from his lips to brighten her day. And making him happy made her happy.

But for how long?

Tentacles of real fear gripped Libby. It was inevitable. He would leave. It wasn't a matter of if, but when.

The only reason Carson hadn't left already was because she'd been careful. She'd played the game well. She'd realized that if she allowed him to know the real Libby Carlyle, he'd have been gone in a flash.

Libby had told Sierra that very thing last night when the two women had split a megasundae at The Chocolate Factory. Sierra had laughed at first but had grown serious when she realized Libby meant every word....

"You really think Carson could walk away from you so easily?" Sierra touched her mouth with the napkin and fixed her gaze on her friend. "From what you've said, it sounds like the guy is crazy about you."

"We get along great." Libby licked the rest of the whipped cream from her spoon before continuing. "But once he gets to know the real me, he'll be gone like that."

As she snapped her fingers Libby could almost see

Carson slamming the door, or worse, closing it with a casual indifference. A knot formed in the pit of her stomach. She forced herself to breathe.

"Once he knows the real you?" Sierra rolled her eyes. "Don't give me that. I know you. I like you. You're a great person and a wonderful friend."

Sierra had always been Libby's staunchest ally, so the support was no surprise. But even while Sierra's words warmed Libby's heart, they couldn't change facts.

"Besides," Sierra added, "he does know you. You've been dating him for over a month."

Libby rested her elbows on the tabletop. She was through with sugar-coating. "Long story short is that I've let Carson believe that I'm a better person than I really am."

Sierra didn't say a word. She only smiled encouragingly and waited for Libby to continue.

"For one thing he thinks I'm a devout Christian." Guilt nagged Libby. Attending church every week with Peggy had started to have an effect. Lying about a relationship with God hadn't bothered her at first. Now it seemed almost…sinful.

Sierra lifted a brow and though not even the merest hint of a smile graced her lips, Libby knew what her friend was thinking.

"I know. It's almost laughable," Libby said. The funny thing was she didn't have the slightest urge to laugh. "God and Libby Carlyle best friends? I'm sure the Big Guy doesn't even know my name."

"God not only knows your name, He loves you very much," Sierra said in a quiet firm voice. The sincerity in her brown eyes was so convincing that if Libby had been less world-weary, she might have been tempted to believe her friend.

Instead Libby shifted her gaze out the window and waved off the sentiment. "Anyway, religion aside, you know how I can be. But Carson thinks I'm sweet, kind, even generous." This time Libby had to laugh. "I may be generous, but I'm rarely kind. And I'm certainly never sweet. You see the problem?"

Sierra's lips pursed together and for a moment it almost appeared she was struggling not to laugh. But when she spoke, her tone was serious. "Maybe it's time you let him see the real you. See what happens from there."

Though the suggestion was what Libby had expected, she knew what following it would mean. "He'll be out the door before I can blink."

"If he doesn't love *you*," Sierra said with unexpected vehemence, "you don't want him anyway."

"I should never have gotten involved with Carson," Libby said almost to herself. "I knew how it would end."

"And he has to love you with his whole heart," Sierra continued as if Libby hadn't spoken. "Or it's not going to be enough to make it through the rough times.''

''No one will ever love me that much,'' Libby said. ''No one ever has, and no one ever will.''

''Libby?''

The masculine voice brought Libby back to the present with a start. She lifted her gaze. Carson stood in front of her, his blue eyes soft and warm.

''You were a million miles away.'' Carson tipped her head back with his fingers. ''What were you thinking?''

Libby's heart picked up speed, the familiar blend of electricity and anticipation coursing through her at his nearness. Her gaze lingered on his beautiful face. ''Actually, I was thinking of doing this—''

She wrapped her arms around Carson's neck and slanted her mouth across his. His lips were soft and warm, just like his eyes, and though for a second she could sense his surprise, his arms reached around her, pulling her close.

He returned the kiss as if it had been months, not days, since their lips had met.

The spicy scent of his cologne filled her nostrils, and the taste of him was so familiar, so beloved that an unexpected rush of emotion brought a hint of tears to her eyes.

Dear God, had she been crazy? Thinking she could ever just be his friend?

"Lib?" Carson took a step back, his eyes searching hers. "Is something wrong?"

Libby blinked back the ridiculous tears, angry at herself for being so emotional.

"Nothing's wrong," Libby said, pleased her voice sounded almost normal. "Unless you count Sunrise being out of scones this morning. Or the fact that I'm coming off an incredibly boring weekend."

"I missed you, too." Carson's lips quirked up in a smile. He reached up and gently cupped her face. "I never realized before that seventy-two hours could seem so long."

"Some friends only see each other every month or so." Libby kept her tone light.

"Well, this friend—" Carson lowered his head and scattered kisses down her neck "—could never go that long."

His kisses sent little arrows of fire shooting through her. But even as she lifted her chin and tilted her head back reveling in the touch of his lips against her skin, Libby couldn't help but remember that not seeing her this weekend had been his choice, not hers.

There had been a music festival Sunday night that Libby had wanted to attend. She'd planned it all in her head, until she could almost picture it. With a warm July breeze caressing their faces she and Carson would listen to jazz, munch on crackers and Brie and sip Merlot. They'd spread a blanket on the ground, and as the night progressed Carson would steal some kisses under the stars.

It would have been a perfectly romantic evening...if he'd just said yes. But he'd turned her down flat. He hadn't given a reason, had just said he was busy that evening.

"What are you talking about? You went all weekend without seeing me," Libby reminded him, stroking the back of his neck with her fingers.

He sighed with pleasure. "That's because you had to work Saturday night."

She ignored the comment. While it was true that helping Peggy at a catering job in Solvang had tied up her Saturday, Carson wouldn't have been free anyway. He'd opened and closed the restaurant that day. But Sunday had been his day off.

"And you had to work Sunday," Libby said her voice deceptively matter-of-fact.

Despite her words, Libby knew better. She'd swung by the restaurant during the supper hour on the pretext of picking up some papers. Not only had Carson been nowhere in sight, the hostess had informed Libby that he hadn't been in all day.

"I didn't work yesterday," Carson said immediately.

"Really?" Libby injected a hint of surprise in her tone. "I guess I just assumed that's why you couldn't go to the concert with me."

Libby tossed the words out like a fisherman baiting a hook and waited patiently for Carson to bite.

"I'd promised to take my nephew to the zoo," Carson said. "Then the family all got together for dinner."

"I didn't know you had a nephew," Libby said. "That must keep your little brother busy—being married, having a child and going to school, too."

Carson chuckled.

Libby frowned. "What's so funny?"

"The thought of Connor being a father." Carson's smile widened. "My little brother can barely take care of himself. I can't imagine him with a wife and child."

"He's not the father?"

"No, he's not." Carson's smile faded. "Seth is Cole's son."

"The brother who went to Africa?" Libby couldn't hide her surprise. She thought back to the conversation when Carson had first mentioned his brothers. "You never told me he'd left a family behind."

Libby couldn't believe Cole's wife could be so self-sacrificing. If she were pregnant and her husband wanted to take a trip half a world away, no matter what the good cause, Libby knew she'd throw a fit. "I can't believe he'd go off and leave her to have the baby alone."

"Becca didn't know she was pregnant until after

Cole had left,'' Carson said after a moment. ''He wouldn't have gone if he'd known. I'm sure of it.''

But he didn't sound sure of it and Libby couldn't help but wonder how two brothers could be so different. She couldn't imagine Carson ever being so selfish. For a brief moment Libby considered telling him that, but she had the feeling Carson wouldn't take her words as a compliment, but rather as a criticism of his brother.

''Do you spend a lot of time with your nephew?'' The minute Libby asked the question she realized how odd it was that she didn't know such a basic thing about Carson's life. But then, she reminded herself that today was the first time Carson had mentioned the boy.

''Not as much as I'd like,'' Carson said. His gaze lingered on Libby. ''Lately it's been hard for me to pull myself away from Santa Barbara.''

Libby slid her hand up his arm. ''Running a restaurant can be very time-consuming.''

His smoldering gaze met hers. ''I wasn't referring to the job.''

Her heart skipped a beat. ''I thought you were a workaholic.''

''I used to be a workaholic,'' he clarified. ''Now I'm a friendaholic. I find myself wanting to spend all my spare time with my friend.''

''Friends,'' Libby corrected.

''Friend,'' Carson said emphatically. He took her

hand and lifted it to his lips. "My very special friend."

Libby's pulse quickened. "Are you saying you wanted to go with me to the music festival?"

"I did," he said. "Very much. All evening I couldn't stop thinking about you."

Libby smiled.

"What about you?" he asked. "Did you miss me?"

Though she probably should keep him guessing, Libby was through with games. From now on she would play it straight. Or at least as straight as she could play it while still pretending to be someone else and living a life that wasn't her own.

"I might have thought about you a few times," Libby admitted with exaggerated reluctance.

"A few?" Carson's dimple flashed. "More than once or twice?"

Libby lifted one shoulder in a slight shrug. "Maybe."

"You know what I think?" Carson smiled. "I think you thought of me a lot. I think you like me a lot, too."

Libby had to smile at the almost boyish arrogance in his tone. "You're acting kind of sure of yourself, mister."

"Are you saying it's not true?"

Libby stood on her tiptoes and, still laughing

kissed him hard on the mouth. "I'm thinking we need to quit talking and get to work."

"I'd rather kiss you," Carson said, pulling her to him.

Libby shrugged, wrapped her arms around his neck and lifted her face to his. "You're the boss."

Chapter Fifteen

"Everything going okay?" Carson leaned over Libby's shoulder and looked at the long list of names.

No, she wanted to snap, everything is not okay. She'd only agreed to hostess this evening because she thought it would give her a chance to be with him. After all, only a little over a week remained before she and Sierra would return to their own lives.

But from the moment she'd walked through the door at five they'd been on a wait. And Carson had been back in the kitchen.

Libby gestured with her head toward the crowded lobby. "If I had a magic wand, I'd make them all disappear."

Carson laughed as if she'd made a joke. He squeezed her shoulder and leaned in close, lowering his voice for her ears only. "We wouldn't want that. Think of all the money we'd lose."

"I don't know about you, but right now it'd be worth it to me." Libby shot a censuring look at a little boy shaking the ficus tree.

Carson stared at her for a long moment, then chuckled and brushed a chaste kiss across her cheek. "Have I told you how much I've missed you?"

A surge of pleasure shot though Libby. Finally things were looking up. A smile tipped her lips and she turned toward him. But Carson was already walking away. Tony, the lead cook, had called in sick and Carson had been stuck helping out in the kitchen. It was dreadfully unfair.

But Libby didn't have time to dwell on the unfairness of life. In fact, it was almost ten before she was able to think of anything beyond which table was opening up next. The wait, which had hovered around two hours for most of the evening, had finally dropped to immediate seating. When the other hostess said she could handle it on her own, Libby didn't argue.

Though she'd skipped dinner, Libby wasn't hungry. She just wanted to get off her aching feet and relax for a few minutes before she headed home.

She checked out the table around the corner from the hostess stand, a small two-top usually reserved for employees. Heaving a sigh of relief that it was open, she pulled out the chair and collapsed.

Her ankle throbbed and her head ached. Pulling a couple of aspirin from her purse, Libby washed them down with the glass of water she been sipping all evening. Her gaze dropped to her stylish high-heeled sandals. But even as she bent over and her fingers reached for the strap, Libby hesitated, afraid if she took the shoes off, she'd never get them on again.

Still, her toes were screaming to be set free and she doubted she'd be able to walk a single step more in the pointy-toed shoes anyway. Throwing caution to the wind, Libby kicked off the sandals. Even if she had to walk barefoot to her car, it'd be worth it.

Reveling in the feel of unrestricted toes, Libby didn't notice Carson approaching until he'd slipped into the seat across from her.

"Great job this evening." He smiled and gave her the thumbs-up. "You and Nora handled the front like a couple of pros."

"Please, enough already." Libby groaned. "I don't want to hear another word about anything even remotely work related. This is the first time I've sat down all evening and I don't want to ruin the moment."

He caught sight of her shoes sitting next to the table and his dimple flashed in his left cheek. "Feet hurt?"

"Actually they feel great." Libby lifted one foot and wiggled her toes. "I'm ready for some dancing. Care to join me?"

His gaze settled on her pink-tipped toes and his smile widened.

"I can tell you're tempted," she said in a teasing tone.

"I'd love to dance with you," he said in a husky voice, his eyes turning dreamy. "Hold you close, move across the floor with you in my arms."

Strains of romantic love songs ran through Libby's head. "Everything here will be pretty much shut down by now." Libby tried not to sound too eager. "But L.A. isn't that far away."

Carson didn't answer immediately but Libby could tell despite the lines of fatigue edging his eyes that he was seriously considering her offer. She held her breath. Heading off to L.A. for a night of dancing and romance would save the evening from being a total waste.

"I'd love to go." Despite the words, regret filled his blue eyes and her hopes plummeted. "But I'm going to have to take a rain check. I've worked sixteen hours today and I'm exhausted."

It was a flimsy excuse. Libby had always believed a person made time for things that were important. And he wasn't the only one plagued by fatigue. A part of her wanted nothing more than to go straight home and sleep until noon. But she was twenty-six, not eighty-six, and sometimes you had to seize the moment.

She decided to give it one more shot and offered

Carson her most enticing smile. "Now you can't be *that* tired. Besides, tomorrow is Sunday. You can sleep in."

Indecision warred on his face. Finally he shook his head. "I can't."

Libby's smile slipped.

"Carson?" A tall thin man whose name Libby couldn't recall peered around the corner. "We need you in the kitchen."

"Be there in a minute," Carson said, making no move to get up.

"But we—"

One glance from Carson stilled the man's protest. He disappeared without another word.

Libby heaved an exasperated sigh. Why couldn't everyone just leave Carson alone? If he hadn't had to cook tonight, he wouldn't be so tired and chances are they'd be headed to L.A. at this very moment. "What's wrong with Tony, anyway?"

"Flu," Carson said. "His wife said he had the stomach flu."

"He looked fine last night," Libby said, remembering how Tony had laughed and joked with some of the waitresses after his shift had ended.

Carson shrugged. "You know how that stuff works. One minute you're fine, the next your head is in the toilet."

Libby wrinkled her nose, not liking the visual image.

"So, back to the dancing," she said. "Are you sure I can't interest you in coming?"

"I wish I could."

Though he was still saying no, a comforting warmth unfolded in Libby's chest at the sincere regret in his voice.

"I might just go home, too." Libby ran her nail across the tabletop. "You're right. Tomorrow will come all too soon."

"Got big plans?" he asked, leaning back in his chair and acting as if he had all the time in the world.

Libby shrugged. "I think I'll just sleep in and take it from there."

Carson paused. "What about church?"

She hesitated.

"Lib?" Carson offered her a smile and she realized he was waiting for an answer.

"I'm not going." She decided to keep her answer simple and to the point. "I don't get much out of church, so I've decided not to bother."

Carson's eyes widened and he opened his mouth to speak, then seemed to think better of it and shut it again.

"Carson?"

Libby shifted her gaze. The tall man from the kitchen was back.

"I just have one quick question." The man spoke quickly. "Joey says he has to leave at eleven but he's scheduled to close—"

"I'll stay and close." Though his words were directed to his employee, Carson's gaze never left Libby's face. "But tell Joey next time he wants to change the schedule, he has to do it in advance."

"Will do." The man shot Libby an apologetic look. "Sorry to interrupt."

The man was out of sight before Carson spoke. "Come with me to church tomorrow."

"Thanks, but no thanks." She flashed him a polite smile.

"C'mon, it'll be fun. I'd like to spend some time with you." Carson reached across the table and took her hand. "I meant what I said earlier. I've missed you."

Libby tried to think of another way to gracefully decline. She'd already told Peggy she wouldn't be attending any more services with her. Although Peggy hadn't liked the idea, she'd reluctantly agreed that Libby was an adult and could make her own decisions.

The problem was, Peggy wasn't Carson. Carson, whose nearness and touch made it impossible for Libby to think clearly. And Libby had missed seeing him so much she would have agreed to go practically anywhere with him.

"It'll be a good time. I promise," he said as if he could sense her weakening resolve. His persuasive tone sent a shiver up her spine.

"A good time?"

"A *very* good time," Carson said, his voice filled with promise.

Libby knew that wasn't possible. She always felt like an outsider. Everyone else seemed to feel renewed and recharged after the hour of worship. All she felt was lonely. "I don't think so."

"Think about it," Carson said, his blue eyes so dark they almost looked black. "You and I sitting side by side, our arms touching, the sweet sounds of music in the air."

The image was so clear, so tempting that Libby was sure she must have misunderstood. "Are we still talking church?"

"Church doesn't have to be boring." Carson took her hand in his and his thumb caressed her palm. "Come with me. Let me show you."

He raised her hand to his lips and placed a kiss in the palm. "Please."

Her skin tingled and an excited quiver filled her stomach. Libby paused, but only for effect. She already knew she couldn't say no. Not to him. Not now.

"Okay, you win. I'll go with you." Other than a few hours of extra sleep, what did she have to lose? If the sermon didn't keep her interest, it wouldn't be the end of the world.

She'd get through tomorrow's service the same way she'd always gotten through boring movies and disappointing theater productions. She'd concentrate on the man at her side.

And when he asked her to spend the rest of the day together, she'd say yes. For no better reason than if she had to suffer through church, he would be her reward.

"What did you think?" Carson plucked a grape from the bunch sitting before him and popped it into his mouth.

For a moment Libby didn't answer. She'd barely given the sermon a second thought.

When they'd returned to Carson's Jeep after the service, he'd uncovered a basket hidden beneath a blanket in the back of the vehicle. It had been filled to the brim with an assortment of fruit and muffins. He'd even included a thermos of her favorite breakfast blend coffee.

They'd driven to a nearby park for a picnic brunch and Libby had pushed all thoughts of the morning's service aside. After all, she had more important things to consider. Like how handsome Carson looked sitting on that red plaid blanket under the blue summer sky.

"The reverend seemed like a nice man," Libby said remembering the warm welcome the gray-haired gentleman had given her when she'd walked through the door on Carson's arm.

"What about his sermon?" Carson pressed. "Did you like it?"

Libby struggled to remember the topic. Something about missions? Haiti? She'd quit listening after the first five minutes and had spent the rest of the time mentally composing her grocery shopping list. "I don't even remember what he talked about."

Shock filled Carson's eyes, then he laughed. "For a minute I thought you were serious."

"I am serious." The truth felt good against Libby's tongue. "I got absolutely nothing out of that sermon."

"You're kidding me."

Libby shook her head and made the decision to go the distance with this honesty thing. She lifted her chin. "In fact, I rarely get anything out of sermons."

She started to add that she'd *never* gotten anything from them, but she knew that wasn't true. A few of the times she'd been with Peggy, a couple of the things the minister said *had* hit home.

"Really?" He exhaled the word.

"Maybe it's because I don't feel particularly close to God," Libby said. "I never have."

The concern in his eyes deepened. "How do you feel about that?"

He said the words slowly and Libby knew that even if it didn't bother her, it bothered him. But the truth was it did bother her. When Sierra and Peggy talked about the comfort they received from their faith, she couldn't help but be envious.

"When I was a little girl, I went to Sunday school every week with my friend. I wanted to believe in God. I wanted that closeness." Libby paused, remembering the incredible loneliness of those years. "But it didn't happen. It just wasn't there. I compare it to finding a guy who you know would be perfect for you, but not being able to make him fall in love with you."

Libby's breath ran out and she realized she'd been rambling. Her cheeks warmed. "I'm sorry. It probably doesn't make much sense and I'm sure that's more than you ever wanted to know."

"Don't apologize." Carson reached over and took her hand. "I understand exactly what you're going through. I went through something similar when I was young. I knew all these Bible verses but, like you, I didn't *know* God. I was even tempted to quit going to church. Then one Sunday I went and the pastor talked about 'mountaintop experiences.'"

The touch of his hand sent tingles racing up her arm and it would have been so easy to end the conversation by closing the distance between them and pressing her lips against his. But as eager as she was for his kisses, Libby had a sudden urge to know what he'd discovered that long-ago Sunday. "'Mountaintop experiences?'"

"I'll give you the condensed version." Carson met

her gaze and smiled. "You can go to church every Sunday and think you're getting nothing out of it. But in fact you are because you're worshiping with other Christians and strengthening your faith bit by bit, week by week. And being there every week has another advantage. It guarantees that you'll be sitting in that pew when that mountaintop experience occurs."

Libby tilted her head and stared at Carson. "Is there champagne in the orange juice?"

Carson laughed and held up a hand. "I'll get to the point. Basically, a mountaintop experience is one of those *aha* moments. It's when the minister says something that hits home, something that speaks to you and brings you closer to God. That's why you have to be there every week. You can never tell when it will happen."

Libby pondered the notion. She'd always assumed God was never there for her but now she wondered if she'd given Him a fair chance.

"Makes sense," she said finally.

"You should give it a try."

"I might," Libby said.

"Did I tell you how pretty you look today?" His gaze flickered briefly over her sleeveless blue dress before returning to her lips.

Libby's smile widened. The discussion was over.

She leaned forward and brushed his lips with hers.

Now it was time for dessert.

Chapter Sixteen

Carson pulled Libby close. The feel of her against him seemed so right. Her silky hair brushed his cheek and he inhaled the scent of her shampoo. Although there were flowers everywhere, the clean fresh fragrance he'd come to associate with Libby Summers was a hundred times sweeter.

Or maybe, he thought as his lips closed over hers, maybe it was because it was part of her. Lately he couldn't seem to get enough of her. The hours they spent together were never long enough. When he wasn't with her, he missed her.

And as her arms looped about his neck and she responded to the kiss, Carson realized that as much as he enjoyed this aspect of their relationship, what he felt for Libby went far beyond sexual attraction.

The thought took him by surprise and for a moment he stilled. Could it be that he was falling in love with Libby?

"Carson?" Libby's eyes were large and very blue in her upturned face. "Is something wrong?"

At first, he didn't realize why she'd even asked the question. The sun was shining overhead, the sky was a brilliant blue and she was in his arms....

Except, he realized, she wasn't anymore. Not really. He'd dropped his arms to his side and her hands now rested on his shoulders rather than around his neck.

Her gaze was puzzled and a hint of worry furrowed her brow.

Carson smiled and kissed her gently. "Nothing is wrong. Actually I was just thinking how perfect it would be if we could spend the whole day together."

"All day?" Her eyes took on a teasing glint and her lips quirked up in a smile. "Don't tell me you're going to play hooky from work."

She was right. He did have work waiting for him in his office. Still...

His gaze lingered on the woman before him. He'd barely seen her this past week and soon she'd be starting back to school. It was hard to know what would happen to their friendship after that.

"Sunday is my day off, remember? And Tony should be back in the kitchen," he said. "So if you're free and if you're interested..."

"I'm available." She lifted one hand from his

shoulder and caressed his cheek with the back of her hand. "But it'll cost you."

Carson smiled. Though he wasn't sure where she was going with this, by the look in her eye he felt sure it was a direction he wanted to go. "How much?"

"Not money," she said with a laugh. "Kisses. Whenever I say 'Carson, kiss me' you have to do it."

"No matter where we're at or what we're doing?"

"Correct." Libby nodded.

"Seems a bit hard-line." Though Carson tried to keep his expression serious, he couldn't quite pull it off. Not with Libby's lips begging to be kissed.

"That's the deal. Take it or leave it," Libby said, a smile tugging at the corners of her mouth.

"Can we start now?" he asked.

Her smile widened, but she held up a hand as he reached for her. "You agree to my terms?"

"I do," he said without hesitation, the words feeling so right on his tongue.

"You're one smart man."

"I'm glad you think so." Carson moved closer. "But those weren't exactly the words I was hoping to hear."

"Carson." Libby's cheeks took on a rosy hue. "Kiss…Tony?"

He paused, not sure if he'd heard correctly.

"Are you trying to change the rules midstream?"

Carson chuckled. "Because if you are, I'm telling you right now, I'm not kissing anyone named Tony."

Libby ignored his teasing tone and her gaze turned serious. "Look behind," she said in a low, terse voice. "Isn't that Tony from the kitchen?"

Carson turned slowly. The playground area was crowded but he spotted his lead cook immediately. Tony was talking to his wife while she pushed a dark-haired toddler on a swing. A knot formed in the pit of his stomach. "That's him."

"I thought he was working today."

Carson glanced down at his watch. Eleven o'clock. Tony should have been at work thirty minutes ago. "He was on the schedule."

Carson couldn't stop the rush of disappointment that flowed through his veins. He'd always tried to be fair to his employees. He'd always treated them with respect and tried to accommodate their requests for time off. All he'd expected was that they would do their job and be honest with him.

"But shouldn't he be…?" Libby's voice trailed off.

"At work?" Carson's voice sounded harsh to his own ears. "I would think so, but I'd better check and be sure."

Not wanting to jump to conclusion, Carson tugged the cell phone from his pocket and called the restaurant. In a matter of minutes, he had his answer.

He flipped the phone closed, slipped it back in his

pocket and reached for the basket. "We'd better get this stuff packed up."

Libby's fingers closed around his arm. "First tell me what they said."

"He called in sick again," Carson said, his voice heavy with disappointment.

"Did they find someone to fill in?"

Carson shook his head.

"I don't understand," Libby said. "Why didn't they call you?"

"They knew how many hours I've been putting in," he said, "and they said they thought they could make do."

"But you're going in anyway, aren't you?" This time the disappointment sounded in her voice.

"I have to," he said. "I know what it's like to work in that kitchen shorthanded. I can't do that to them."

"I understand," Libby said reluctantly. "Although I do think you would have had more fun spending the day with me."

"No doubt about that." Carson couldn't help but respond to her impish smile. For a moment he was tempted to call the restaurant and say he wouldn't be in. His hand slid into his pocket and closed around the phone, but he stopped himself just in time. If he was working short, he'd want someone to come in and help.

With Libby's assistance he loaded up the basket,

folded the blanket and started toward the Jeep in record time. But halfway up the path, Carson paused, knowing he'd left unfinished business behind.

"Could you wait here for me?" He placed the basket on the ground at Libby's feet. "I'll only be a minute."

Libby's gaze turned quizzical. "Did we forget something?"

"Actually," Carson said, "I need to talk to Tony. And now is as good a time as any."

"What are you going to do?" Her voice was soft and troubled.

"What do you think?"

"I don't know." Her gaze remained watchful. "That's why I asked."

Carson drew a deep breath and exhaled it. He hated to lose a man who'd been a good employee up to this point, but he would not—could not—put up with this behavior.

"I'm going to fire him," he said at last.

"After you find out what's going on, right?"

"He lied. At this point, the why is irrelevant," Carson said. "There's no excuse. Lying is something I won't tolerate."

Lying is something I won't tolerate.

Libby thought about bringing up the subject on the drive home, but she wasn't sure what she'd say. That honesty was often overrated? That there could be a good reason why someone would lie? Or maybe, "Oh, by the way, I'm not who you think I am." Libby could only imagine the response.

"I know you're in a hurry to get to the restaurant," Libby said as he turned on her street. "You can just drop me off in front."

"I think I can spare an extra five minutes." Carson winked and wheeled the Jeep into the driveway.

Shutting off the engine, he got out and opened the passenger door for her.

"You're such a gentleman," Libby said, stepping down to the concrete with the assistance of his hand.

He grinned and shut the door. "I try."

"Don't work too hard today." Instead of starting immediately toward the house, Libby leaned back against the vehicle door, reluctant to see him leave.

"I wish it could have been different." Regret filled Carson's gaze. The look told her that cutting their time together short was as hard on him as it was on her. Though the knowledge didn't take away her disappointment, it did make her feel slightly better.

He sighed. "I wish we could have spent the rest of the day—"

"Shh." Libby leaned over and pressed her fingers against his lips. "I wish that, too, but you need to go. I know that."

"Can I call you later?"

"If you want." Libby lifted one shoulder in a nonchalant shrug. "But don't make it too late. I'm a working girl and I need my beauty sleep. My slave-driver boss makes me come to work at the crack of dawn.''

Carson grinned at her irreverent tone. The tension in his face eased. ''Libby, Libby. What am I going to do with that mouth of yours?''

''I'm surprised you need to ask.'' She took a step forward, closing the distance between them. Her noble intention to let him get on his way was forgotten in a less noble need to feel his arms around her. ''Kiss me, Carson. One more time…''

''Isn't Carson going to be eating with us?'' Becca frowned at the sight of only three place settings on the dining room table.

''Not today.'' Elaine Davies adjusted the flowers she'd bought in from the garden.

Though Elaine didn't elaborate, Becca wasn't about to let the subject drop. Up until a couple of months ago it had been unthinkable for Carson to miss a Sunday dinner. Every week, after church, he'd head straight to San Rafael. While Becca and his mother prepared the food and set the table, Carson would play with Seth and update them on his week.

Becca had grown used to Carson's Sunday visits. In fact, she'd started thinking of Sunday as *their* day. Because after lunch, Seth would nap and Elaine would shoo them out of the house, saying that Seth would never get any sleep with the two of them yakking and laughing.

It had been so much fun, Becca thought wistfully. For those few hours she'd forget that she had a child and responsibilities and just enjoy herself.

Though in the beginning her feelings for Carson had been merely sisterly, lately that had started to change. She'd begun to see Carson as a man, and she'd found herself wishing that he'd treat her less like a kid sister and more like a real woman. Her feelings were ironic considering for the longest while she could scarcely bear to look at him.

Carson had been a painfully vivid reminder of what she'd lost. His brother had been Becca's first love. The moment she'd laid eyes on Cole in the college library, she'd known he was the man for her. If she had the chance Becca knew she'd be with him all over again. She and Cole had connected on every level. And even if he hadn't said he loved her, she'd been convinced that he did.

Her gaze slid to the little towheaded boy sitting on the floor playing with a stack of blocks. Becoming a single mother so early in life wasn't something she'd planned, but she wouldn't give up her son for anything in the world.

But she wanted more for him than she'd had growing up. She'd never known her father, and though her mother had tried, one person couldn't do the job of two. Becca wanted Seth to know a father's love. And

Carson was the perfect candidate for the job. He already loved Seth, and even if he wasn't his biological father, he was as close as she could come.

It was a perfect solution unless…

"Is Carson seeing someone?" Becca asked abruptly.

Elaine paused and adjusted the already perfectly arranged bouquet. "He might have said something about a new friend."

Becca swallowed a groan. She loved Elaine, she really did. But the woman's protectiveness of her sons could be trying at times. "How good a friend?"

"I don't know, honey," Elaine said.

"He likes her a lot, doesn't he?"

"Perhaps," Elaine said. "I mean, he hasn't said much, but the times he has mentioned her, I can hear affection in his voice. It reminds me of how Cole used to speak of you."

Becca hated it when Elaine brought up Cole. Initially thinking of him had made her feel sad. Now all she felt was anger. Anger that he could so easily leave her. Anger that he would put himself in a dangerous situation with no regard for those who loved him. And most of all, angry that he'd died and left her when she's needed him most.

Swallowing the lump in her throat, Becca shoved the thought of Cole aside and forced herself to concentrate on the present. "Do you think it's serious?"

"I don't honestly know." Elaine shifted her attention from the flowers to the tableware. "All I know is he seems happy."

"But what about Seth?" Anger at the unfairness of the whole situation rose inside her breast. "If Carson marries this woman, where does that leave my son?"

Elaine lifted her gaze, surprise flickering in the blue depths. "Carson loves Seth," she said softly. "That will never change."

"Sure it will," Becca countered. "He'll get busy with his own life. He won't have time for Seth or for me."

"Oh, honey." Elaine crossed the room. "I know you wish there could be something more between you and Carson—"

"My son needs a father," Becca blurted out, surprising Elaine with her candor. "And if Carson doesn't want the job, I guess I'm going to find someone who does."

Chapter Seventeen

Libby took a sip of her drink and breathed a contented sigh. She loved nothing better than sitting on her veranda, listening to music and relaxing.

"Want some company?"

Libby jerked her gaze toward the sound, her heart pounding in her chest. The voice was low and husky and immediately familiar.

She smiled even before the tall broad-shouldered figure stepped out from the shadows. "Carson. What a surprise."

"I hope a pleasant one," he said with a boyish smile, the dimple flashing in his cheek as he started up the steps. He paused at the top and gestured toward the chair next to Libby. "May I join you?"

"Please do." Libby clicked the remote, the volume on the CD player lowering until the Puccini aria was a mere whisper on the wind. Libby lifted an empty flute and raised a questioning brow. "Can I interest you in a drink?"

Carson didn't answer immediately. He merely stared, his expression inscrutable. "Expecting someone?"

"I've been stood up," Libby said with an easy smile. She'd brought out an extra glass, on the off chance Sierra might stop by. "If she were coming, she'd be here by now."

"In that case—" Carson flashed a smile that made her heart flip-flop "—I'd love one."

He took a seat, but when she reached for the bottle he firmly removed it from her grasp. "You don't have to wait on me."

After pouring the glass half-full, Carson brought the bottle close and studied the label before placing it back on the table.

"Great year." He brought the glass to his lips and took a sip. "Wonderful flavor."

"It's one of my favorites." Libby smiled, glad to see he could appreciate a good vintage. Taking another sip, Libby studied Carson over the top of the glass. She was glad he'd stopped by tonight, but she wished he would have called ahead.

She glanced down at her denim shorts and sleeveless cotton top. While the casual attire was perfectly fine for sitting on the porch, drinking and gabbing with a girlfriend, she would have picked something a little prettier to wear if she'd known Carson was coming over.

"I didn't expect to find you at the main house," Carson said conversationally. "I went to your place first but it was dark. But since your car was there and the lights were on up here—"

"You decided to take a chance," Libby said.

"And it paid off." He lifted his glass in a brief toast before taking a sip.

"I'm glad you've got an adventurous spirit." She leaned back in her chair and fanned herself with a magazine.

"And I'm glad you were home," he said. "Or at least on the property."

"Me, too."

Carson glanced toward the open screen door leading into the house. "Is the lady of the house home?"

"Mrs. Carlyle lives in France," Libby said matter-of-factly, popping a grape in her mouth.

Carson's brow furrowed. "But she still keeps Peggy on—I mean your mother—as a housekeeper? That doesn't make sense."

Libby thought quickly. Maybe this would be the time to tell him that this was *her* house. After all, next week at this time she'd be back to her old life and he'd know the truth then anyway.

She opened her mouth to speak but the words stuck in her throat. Though Libby wanted to come clean, the memory of how he'd reacted to learning about

Tony's lie was all too fresh in her mind. And telling him now would ruin what promised to be a lovely evening. Yes, she had to tell him. But not tonight.

"Her daughter stays here off and on," Libby said. "In fact, I thought she was coming home tonight. But I must have gotten the dates mixed up."

"If you'd feel more comfortable, we could go to your house." Carson glanced in the direction of the cottage.

"Don't worry about it," Libby said with a dismissive wave.

"If you're sure." Though a flicker of doubt lingered in Carson's gaze, he stayed seated.

"Positive." Libby gestured to the plate of cheese and fruit. "Can I interest you in a snack?"

They sat in the quiet darkness for the longest time, talking about life and fighting over the chocolate-dipped strawberries.

A languid warmth filled her limbs and Libby wondered what Carson would do if she asked him to kiss her.

Her lips curved upward. Who was she kidding? He'd already given his answer. The way his gaze had lingered on her mouth told her there was more than eating strawberries on his mind.

But before Libby could cluck or even say "Kiss me, Carson" in her most enticing voice, his attention strayed to the door leading into the house.

"This is a beautiful home," he said. "And, judging from what I see from here, it's as nice on the inside.''

Though her mother had never liked the stately Victorian, it was the only home Libby had ever known and she was immensely proud of it. ''Would you like a tour?''

''That'd be great.'' Carson's eyes lit up. ''If you're sure the owner won't care. I don't want you to get in any trouble on my account.''

''She won't care.'' Libby shoved back her chair and stood. She must have moved too quickly because the lightheadedness that had plagued her all afternoon returned with a vengeance. Thankfully after a second or two of standing perfectly still, the feeling passed. She moved to the door and held it open. ''Follow me.''

Libby gave Carson the grand tour, starting in the completely stocked wine cellar and ending in an attic filled with an assortment of items her mother had left behind when she'd moved to France.

''What's under there?'' Carson pointed to a far wall. A large gilt-edged picture frame peeped out from underneath a swath of white sheeting.

Libby shrugged. ''No idea.''

Actually she didn't have a clue about most of the items that were stored in this part of the house. She couldn't remember the last time she'd been in the attic. Standing there now, at the peak of the roof, she realized why she never came up here. The air was stale and musty and the place hot as an oven. Perspiration dotted Libby's brow and slithered down her back. Her stomach lurched.

"Shall we take a look?" Carson moved toward the picture and, apparently taking Libby's silence for assent, removed the drape. He took a step back and stared. "Impressive."

Libby's eyes widened and she felt as if she'd been socked in the stomach. It was a family portrait. *Her* family portrait. Though her mother's hair was shorter, Stella Carlyle hadn't changed much in the twenty-five years since this portrait had been painted. Standing next to her was Libby's father. It was easy to see why her dad had been so popular with the ladies. His dark black hair and brilliant blue eyes were striking. In his arms was a baby girl dressed in white lace. She had no hair, bright blue eyes and an enchanting toothless smile.

They looked so happy. But Libby knew all too well how looks could be deceiving. A familiar ache filled her heart.

"You're right. It is a beautiful frame." Libby wiped the perspiration from her brow and moved toward the stairs, anxious to get out of the sweltering heat.

"I wasn't talking about the frame." Carson still stood by the portrait, not seeming in any hurry at all. "I was referring to the family. They're a nice-looking bunch. Are they the home's owners?"

"Yes, they are." Libby steadied herself with a hand on the banister. "Let's go downstairs. It's too hot and stuffy up here."

"Really? I hadn't noticed."

Carson carefully replaced the drape over the portrait and followed Libby down the stairs to the parlor. "This is a beautiful house. It reminds me of you, so classy and elegant."

Libby turned to find Carson directly behind her, his eyes dark and intense. A ripple of awareness traveled up her spine. Libby's breath fell outward on a soft sigh as his mouth covered hers. How was it possible that she'd lived twenty-six years without ever feeling this, without ever knowing how much you could love someone? Libby didn't hold back. She put all her emotion, all her love, in her kiss.

His arms tightened around her and it seemed so right to be in his arms. The breeze from the front screen door blew her hair across her face but Libby barely noticed. Nothing mattered except Carson and the closeness.

He broke off the kiss and stepped back, his breath coming in ragged puffs. "I should go."

Libby swayed slightly, but then leaned forward and laced her fingers through his hair. "C'mon, Carson," she said in a low husky voice. "Don't be chic—"

Before she could finish, his lips were once again on hers, this time firm and demanding.

Libby buried her fingers in the silky softness of his hair and forgot about everything except how wonderful it was to be in the arms of the man she loved. She wasn't sure how long they kissed. She only knew that when he pulled back, it wasn't nearly long enough.

"Will you go upstairs with me?" he whispered against her throat.

"Why?" Libby hated answering one question with another, but he wasn't making any sense. "Other than the attic, there's nothing but bedrooms up there."

"I know," he said.

The realization of what he was asking hit her full force. Libby's heart pounded in her chest. "I don't know what to say."

He leaned forward and kissed her full on the mouth. "Say yes."

Chapter Eighteen

Carson died a thousand deaths waiting for Libby's response. Normally not an impetuous person, he knew this course of action ranked right up there with jumping out of a plane without a parachute.

But for the first time Carson could understand why his brother had taken all those risks. There was something exhilarating about throwing caution to the wind and going with the moment.

Libby was so beautiful, so warm and so full of life. He wanted her more than he'd ever wanted a woman.

They'd grown close these past few months, closer than he'd ever believed possible. He enjoyed her company and her kisses and he knew he'd enjoy taking the next step. They were both adults. There really wasn't any reason he and Libby couldn't be intimate.

Other than the fact that it was wrong.

Carson ignored the brief attack of doubt. In an ideal world, intimacy would only be found in the marriage bed. Of course, in an ideal world, his brother would still be alive.

"I can't."

The words were barely audible and so soft Carson wondered if he'd only imagined them. But when Carson saw the regret on her face, he realized with a sinking heart that the words had come from her. "You can't?"

"In fact, I think you'd better go." She raised her hand to her head and briefly closed her eyes. "Now."

Carson pulled her toward him, linking his arms lightly around her waist. He lifted one hand and brushed the hair back from her face. For the first time he noticed a paleness beneath Libby's tan. "Lib, are you okay?"

When she lifted her head, her blue eyes were glittery bright. "Carson, please just go."

"Why?"

"Because if you don't, I'm going to be sick all over you."

Carson reached up and placed the back of his hand against Libby's forehead. "Libby, darling, you're burning up."

"I don't feel so good." Libby could feel the tears pushing at her lids. From the time she'd been a little girl, she'd had a tendency to cry when she was sick.

But she'd learned early to suppress the tears and put on a brave face. Like her mother always said, no one likes being around a crybaby.

She turned from Carson and blinked rapidly. "You'd better go."

"I'm not going anywhere. Not until I'm sure you're okay." His fingers gently took her chin and turned her face back to his.

The sudden look of tenderness brought fresh tears to her eyes. "I'll be fine." Libby's smile wobbled. "I just want to lie down."

"That makes sense." Carson took his hands away from her face, resting them lightly on the curves of her shoulders, putting a subtle distance between them. "I'll take you home."

Libby shook her head. "I think I'll just stay here."

She couldn't have him taking her back to the cottage. Contaminating Peggy's living quarters with her germs made no sense. Besides, she wanted to spend the night in her own house.

"Are you sure?" Carson's voice was filled with concern.

If she'd felt better, his kindness would have been touching. Instead she just wanted him to go. Needed him to go. Her stomach lurched and Libby knew she was only seconds away from disaster.

With a strangled gasp, she shoved him aside and ran into the bathroom, slamming the door behind her.

Libby stayed by the toilet until the trembling in

her legs stopped and she was sure there was nothing left in her stomach. After rinsing her mouth and brushing her teeth, Libby gathered the little strength she had left and opened the door.

Carson sat on the small settee in the hall. He rose to his feet, concern etched on his brow. "How are you feeling?"

"Better." The walls in the old house were paper-thin and Libby realized suddenly he'd heard everything. She could feel her face warm. "You didn't have to stay."

"I couldn't leave, not with you sick."

"I can take care of myself," she said with a half smile, remembering all the times she'd had to fend for herself when she'd been ill.

"I know you can," he said with a soft smile. "You're one tough cookie. But just because you can, doesn't mean you should have to. We all like to be babied when we're sick."

Tears slipped down Libby's cheeks. She hurriedly brushed them away but they were coming so fast she couldn't keep up. "I'm sorry. I'm not usually so—"

"Shh." Carson reached up and cradling her face in his large hands, brushed her tears back with his thumbs. He wrapped his arms around her and pressed her head to his chest. "You don't have to explain. If it makes you feel better to cry, you go ahead. All I want is for you to feel good enough to cluck again."

One smile was all it took. The tears began to fall

in earnest and Libby let them come. She soaked the front of his shirt, but he didn't seem to mind. He crooned comforting words and stroked the back of her head as if she were a small child.

Finally when she could cry no more, she raised her head and sniffed. "I think I need a tissue."

He pulled a wadded-up piece of tissue from his pocket. "It may not look the best, but it's clean."

"Thank you." She took it gratefully and blew her nose. Her stomach no longer churned and her skin felt clammy rather than hot. But her head ached and exhaustion threatened to overtake her. "I'll just pick up outside—"

"I already did that," he said.

"But when—?"

"When you were in the bathroom," he said. "It didn't take long."

"That was so incredibly sweet." The tears she'd thought were all spent once again filled her eyes.

He winked. "Anytime."

"I must look horrible." She lifted a trembling hand to her face, knowing her skin had to be blotchy and her eyes swollen.

He clasped her hand in his, the warmth and strength of his grasp reassuring. "You look beautiful."

Though he said the words with utmost confidence, she'd caught a glimpse of herself in the bathroom mirror when she'd brushed her teeth. "I don't think so."

"Libby, sweetheart," he said with a gentle smile. "You're always beautiful in my eyes."

Even if it wasn't true, it was kind. But then Carson was a nice man. An honest man. A decent man. A man that didn't deserve to be lied to. Once again the tears welled up. "I need to lie down."

"Sure you don't want to go home?"

She started to tell him she *was* home then stopped herself. "Positive."

Suddenly Libby found herself swept up in his arms.

"What do you think you're doing?" she asked, more because it seemed the thing to say, than out of any real curiosity.

"I'm taking you to bed," he said.

She didn't have the energy to argue. Leaning her head against his chest, she listened to the comforting beat of his heart as he climbed the steps to her room.

"Second door on the right," she said when he reached for the doorknob of the room closest to the stairs.

She could sense his question, even though he didn't say a word. "The second one is the guest bedroom."

Actually it was the truth. She wasn't sure what personal items she had left out in her own bedroom so for tonight she'd sleep in the guest room.

With her still in his arms, he pulled back the sheets and set her gently on the bed. "What can I get you?"

"Nothing," she said, eyeing the soft down-filled pillows with longing.

His gaze narrowed and he leaned forward, touching her forehead with his cheek. "You still have a fever."

"I'm fine."

"Let me get you some aspirin—"

"I'm fine, Carson, really." Libby grabbed his hands. "Thank you so much for taking care of me. I can't tell you how much I appreciate it."

"What else can I do?" He looked around the room. "Can I bring you some water or juice? Or maybe some soda?"

"I just want to go to sleep," Libby said. "I'm sure when I wake up tomorrow I'll be fine."

"I could stay," he said. "Sleep on the couch. Just be here if you need anything?"

"There's no need," she said. "Peggy—I mean, my mother—will be home before long. She can get me whatever I need. You go home and get some sleep."

He hesitated for a long moment. "Okay, I'll go. But only if you promise to call me if you need anything. Deal?"

Libby smiled at the seriousness of his expression. "I promise."

"You'd better call."

"I've already told you I will."

Carson walked to the door and turned, his gaze searching hers. "I had a wonderful evening."

"Yeah, right." In spite of her splitting headache Libby had to chuckle. "It's loads of fun hanging out with a sick person, especially one who cries all over your shirt."

"I like being with you," Carson said, the honesty ringing true in his voice. "I want to be there for you when you're sick. I know you'd do the same for me."

Though Libby had always thought of herself as a basically selfish person, she realized with a start that she would gladly take care of Carson when he was sick. That's the way it should be when you loved someone.

Of course Carson hadn't said the *L* word. But everyone knew that actions speak louder than words. And Carson's actions tonight had definitely said love.

Chapter Nineteen

Carson had barely pulled his front door closed when his cell phone rang. He grabbed it from his pocket, cursing his decision to leave Libby. Obviously, something had gone terribly wrong or she wouldn't be calling.

But when he glanced at the caller ID, it wasn't Libby's number staring back at him, but his mother's. A call this late in the evening from his mother could only mean one thing.

"Mom, what's up?" Carson tried to keep his voice level, even though fingers of icy fear were climbing up his spine. "Is Seth—?"

"He's fine," his mother said immediately, as if knowing the direction his thoughts had taken. "Both he and Becca are fast asleep."

Carson released the breath he didn't even realize

he'd been holding. Over the past two years there'd been numerous late-night visits to the emergency room for Seth's asthma. So many in fact, that he'd lost count. But it would never be routine. Seeing someone you love struggle to breathe was scary. Thankfully a new medication regime seemed to be helping and the trips had gotten fewer.

"When I saw your number on my caller ID my first thought was that Seth had had another attack," Carson said, wandering into the kitchen and opening the refrigerator.

"I hope I didn't wake you."

"Actually, I'd just walked through the door when the phone rang."

"You did?" Surprise sounded in his mother's voice. "Where were you?"

"I was with Libby." Her pale face flashed before him and he wondered if he should give her a call when he got off the phone, just to make sure she was okay. "My friend?"

The word seemed so inadequate. But it was the "official" status of their relationship.

"I remember," his mother said, her voice sounding strange, not like her at all. "In fact, that's part of the reason why I called."

"You want to talk about Libby?" Carson grabbed a bottle of water and shut the refrigerator door. "I don't understand what there is to talk about."

"Becca is on the warpath." His mother spoke

matter-of-factly. "She's upset that you're dating this Libby person."

Carson groaned. This only confirmed his suspicions that Becca had started taking his brotherly friendliness for something more. "She'll just have to get over it."

"She says she's worried about Seth."

"Worried about him how?" Adrenaline flowed through Carson's veins like an awakened river. "I thought you told me he was okay."

"He is," his mother said quickly. "But Becca thinks you won't have time for him now that you have this new relationship."

Carson's heart settled back to a normal rhythm.

"She doesn't need to worry," Carson said, uncapping the bottle of water and taking a drink. "I love Seth. I'll always be there for him."

"Becca wants him to have a father," his mother said. "She thinks he needs one."

"She should have thought about that before she let Cole go to Africa," Carson said, the unexpected sentiment taking him by surprise."

"Honey, that's not fair," she said with a sigh. "None of us wanted him to go."

But Carson wasn't interested in wasting another minute discussing Becca and her ridiculous fears. Not when he was so worried about Libby.

"I've told her I'll be there for Seth. But Becca has

to face facts. Cole is gone," Carson said flatly. "And that means Seth will grow up without a father."

"Not if Becca has anything to say about it. She's determined he *will* have a father," his mother repeated. "And, she practically said that if you don't want the job, she'll find someone who will."

A tense silence enveloped the phone line. "You don't think she'd turn to Jimmy Bellows, do you?"

"No. She knows he's no good." Despite the forceful words, his mother's voice didn't exude much confidence.

Last year Becca's old boyfriend from high school had started coming around. Until she'd made it clear she wasn't interested. Still, Jimmy just lived down the road in Carpinteria and Carson knew the guy would come running if Becca gave him the slightest indication she'd changed her mind.

"But I have to say I've never seen Becca act so irrational," his mother added. "What if she takes Seth away and we never see him?"

"What do you want me to do?" Carson raked his fingers through his hair. "Marry Becca so she doesn't go back to her old boyfriend?"

"Carson." His mother's tone turned sharp. "Don't put words in my mouth. I'm just concerned. Seth is my grandson and your nephew. I want the best for the boy. Your brother would be furious if we didn't do what was best for his son...and for Becca."

On that count there was no disputing his mother's

words. "So you really think she's serious about finding a guy?"

"I do," his mother said. "And I don't believe this is all about Seth. I think she's lonely."

"I'll talk to her," Carson said.

"What are you going to say?" A thread of curiosity replaced the tension in his mother's voice.

"I don't know," Carson answered honestly. "Other than what she should already know, that we love Seth and that we'll always be there for both of them."

"What if she doesn't listen?"

"We'll just have to pray that she does." It wasn't a great answer. Or even a good one. But at the moment it was the only hope Carson had.

"I've had it with women." Brian entered the office and slammed the door shut behind him. He strode across the room to Carson's desk like a man possessed. "If I ever say again that I'm thinking of settling down, just shoot me. Put me out of my misery right then and there."

Carson paused, trying to recall when Brian had ever said anything about settling down. He shrugged and shifted his gaze from the computer to his friend. "Good morning to you, too."

"Weren't you listening?" Brian plopped down into the chair next to the desk and shot Carson a disgusted look. "My life is in shambles. And there is *nothing* good about this morning, nothing at all."

"Did Bambi break up with you?" Carson lifted a brow, trying to keep a smile from his lips.

"Bambi?" Brian recoiled. "I've never dated anyone named—"

The smile on Carson's face stopped Brian's words. "Oh, I get it. You're making a joke. Forgive me if I don't laugh."

"C'mon, Brian, loosen up."

"Loosen up?" Brian snorted. "Just wait until someone you love cheats on you and then I'll see if you still feel so smug."

Though Brian had been whining about his girlfriends for years, Carson realized suddenly that this time was different. The hurt in his eyes and the pain in his friend's voice were all too real and he'd actually used the word *love* in a sentence.

"Who is she?" Carson shoved a stack of papers aside and gave Brian his full attention. It seemed odd that he had to ask. Normally Brian talked about his women ad nauseam, but he'd been strangely silent the past month.

Brian heaved a sigh that stopped just short of being melodramatic. "It's Audra."

"Audra?" Carson straightened in the chair. "I didn't know you two were even dating."

"It's not surprising," Brian said. "You've been so

hung up on luscious Libby that I could have been dating a monkey and you'd never have noticed.''

Carson laughed at the image, but quickly sobered when Brian didn't join in.

''What happened?'' Carson struggled to remember what Brian had said when he'd first walked through the door. ''She…cheated on you?''

For one crazy second Carson wondered if Brian had heard about the offer Audra had made him and if that was what this was all about. But he immediately dismissed the notion. Brian and Audra hadn't even been dating back then. Besides, nothing had happened.

''She told me she couldn't see me Saturday night because she had some company party to attend,'' Brian said. ''I thought it was odd she didn't invite me, but I didn't say anything.''

''That's why you think she's been cheating?'' Carson asked. ''Because she didn't invite you to a party?''

''No.'' Brian heaved an exasperated sigh. ''And let's get one thing straight. I don't *think* she's been cheating, I *know* she has. The night of the supposed party, a couple of friends invited me to go clubbing with them in L.A. I couldn't believe it when I saw her on that dance floor. And before you say something about it being all innocent, let me tell you she was all over the guy.''

Carson paused, visualizing the scene. If he'd been

in Brian's position and it had been Libby with another guy... He shoved the thought aside. Thankfully he could trust Libby to be honest with him. "Did you talk to her?"

"Not that night," Brian said. "But yesterday I asked her how the party was and she made up a bunch of lies."

Carson shrugged and shook his head. "That surprises me. I thought she really liked you."

"It surprised me, too," Brian said. "But it only confirmed what my father always said—women are cheats and liars and you're a fool to ever trust them."

At that moment, Carson couldn't help but feel sorry for his friend. It was obvious Brian had truly cared for Audra. And, not only had he cared for her, he'd dared to put his faith in her.

An image of Libby and her clear, direct gaze flashed before Carson. She didn't pull any punches or hide behind pretense.

Libby Summers was a woman who was honest to a fault.

A woman a man could trust.

A woman a man could love...

Chapter Twenty

Though it was only midmorning, the day was already warm and Libby sipped her ginger ale, thankful for the large trees shading the veranda from the sun.

"Sure you don't want a scone?" Sierra lifted the bag bearing the Sunrise Coffee Company logo and jiggled it enticingly. "They're fresh out of the oven."

Libby shook her head, not the least bit tempted. Her stomach might be growling but she wanted to play it safe. Until she was sure the nausea was gone for good, it would be bland drinks and soda crackers for her.

"Have you been able to keep any food down?" Sierra took a sip of coffee and brought a bite of the oatmeal scone to her mouth.

"I had a couple of crackers this morning." Libby wrapped her hands around the glass. "If I feel better this afternoon, I may try some dry toast. But I don't dare move too fast. No way do I want a repeat performance of last night.''

"I hate throwing up." Sierra shuddered. "Yuck."

"The only thing worse is throwing up when you have a guy out in the hall listening." Libby's lips curved up in a wry smile.

"It's not exactly a top-ten romantic moment," Sierra agreed.

"So true," Libby said.

But the moment the word passed her lips, she wondered if she'd been too quick to agree. Because the more she thought about it, the more she realized that the gentle kindness Carson had shown in her hour of need was incredibly romantic. More romantic than a bushel of long-stemmed roses or boxes of the finest chocolates.

The jarring ring of the phone broke Libby's reverie. She frowned. "I wonder who that could be?"

Sierra smiled. "It's probably someone from the restaurant asking you to help out this evening."

"Yeah, right." Libby picked up the cordless phone lying next to the bag of scones and promptly dismissed the possibility. She'd made it clear when she'd called in that she was definitely out for the whole day. "Hello."

"Libby?"

"Carson." Her smile widened at the sound of the familiar voice and she gave Sierra a wink. "I hope you're not calling to ask me to come into work, because I'd hate to have to turn you down.''

"You're safe," Carson said in that low, deep voice that made her pulse quicken. "I did call to ask you something, but I promise it doesn't have a thing to do with the job.''

"Really?" Libby straightened in her chair. "I'm intrigued.''

"It's nothing that exciting." Carson laughed. "I was just wondering if you felt up to a little company tonight?''

Libby thought quickly. Sierra had mentioned that she and Maddie would be spending the evening at the cottage, so having Carson hang out with her there wouldn't be an option. And she knew he'd find it odd if she suggested they spend time at her "employer's house.''

"What did you have in mind?" Libby asked in a light, airy tone.

"I'm open to suggestions," Carson said. "I don't care where we go or what we do. I just want to see you and make sure you're really okay.''

Warmth flooded Libby at his concern. "My mother is having some company over this evening so things will be a little hectic around the house. I could meet you somewhere?''

"I've got a better suggestion," Carson said. "How about I come by around seven and pick you up?''

"It's a plan." Anticipation coursed through Libby.

Last night she'd been too sick to care if he was around or not. Now that she felt better, she couldn't wait to see him again. "See you at seven."

Clicking off the phone, Libby leaned back in her seat with a satisfied sigh. "That was Carson. He wants to see me."

"What a surprise," Sierra said dryly. She placed her glass of tea on the table and studied Libby with a speculative gaze. "Is tonight the night?"

"For what?" To her horror, Libby felt her face warm.

"For telling him who you really are," Sierra said, clearly puzzled by Libby's reaction. "Unless you're planning to just pull a disappearing act this weekend?"

"Sierra." A hint of reproach colored Libby's words. "You know I could never do that to him."

"I'm not saying you *should,* only that you *could.*" Sierra countered in a reasonable tone. "That girl whose place you took should be back from France, so it's not like they really need you or anything."

But Carson needs me.

Libby hugged the sentiment close, unsure if it was true or just wishful thinking.

"I'm just trying to help you out," Sierra continued. She shifted her gaze to the green expanse of lawn and a pensive look stole over her features. "Believe me, I know how unpleasant the 'coming clean' process can be."

"I take it Matt is still angry?" Libby asked in a cautious tone. Sierra's own summer romance had come to an abrupt halt several weeks ago, but though the lingering pain in her eyes spoke volumes, Sierra had said very little about the matter. "Has he even called?"

"No." Sierra shook her head. "And I don't think he will. But that's okay. If he didn't want me because I have a child, he's not the right man for me."

"That's the spirit," Libby said, patting her hand. Sierra's devotion to her daughter was one of the qualities that Libby admired most.

"The funny thing is, it still hurts," Sierra said in a low voice. "Despite knowing I'm better off without him, having him walk away like that when I thought he cared…"

Her voice trailed off and Libby's heart clenched. Sierra had endured more than her share of pain, but this time Libby feared she'd been responsible for this bout of heartache.

"Changing places was supposed to have been fun," Libby murmured almost to herself. "I don't know how it went so wrong."

"We forgot there were other people involved." Sierra broke off another piece of scone but instead of eating it, she crumbled it between her fingers.

"You're being too kind. There's no need to spare my feelings," Libby said. "Tell it like it is. *I* never considered the feelings of others. This was my crazy scheme, not yours."

Sierra shook her head. "I'm not going to let you play the martyr. If you remember, I was the one who pushed you to go through with it. I couldn't wait to live a life of luxury for the summer."

Libby smiled. "Was it as good as you imagined?"

"In many ways," Sierra said, a tiny smile hovering on her lips. "I loved the freedom of being a business owner, of being able to come and go as I pleased. I liked going out to eat and ordering what I wanted, instead of what was the cheapest. And I have to admit, I adored your car."

"There are perks to having money," Libby admitted. "The BMW is definitely one of them."

"Would *you* do it again?" Sierra asked suddenly.

"Let you have the roadster?" Libby put a finger to her lips and pretended to ponder the question. "Not in a million years."

"I'm not talking about cars," Sierra said in an even tone, keeping her gaze focused on Libby. "Would you make the switch if you had it to do over again?"

Libby thought of the long hours and the penny-pinching she'd had to get used to these past few months. She wouldn't regret having those things out of her life. But then she remembered the friendships she'd made and the good feeling she'd gotten from knowing people could like her for who she was, and not just for what she had. She'd taken risks and opened herself up to others, especially Carson. And when it all fell apart, as it surely would, she wouldn't waste a moment on regrets.

"In a heartbeat." Libby lifted her glass of ginger ale to her lips and shot Sierra a wink. "But this time I'd keep the roadster."

They laughed together and talked for a few minutes longer before Sierra headed back to the cottage to pick up Maddie.

Libby watched her friend descend the porch steps and turn in the direction of the little house at the back of the property. Sierra walked with long, confident strides, her head held high. No one seeing her would ever guess all she'd been through. Sierra was a survivor and an inspiration to Libby.

Goodness knew she needed inspiration. Her confrontation with Carson was still to come.

Last night Libby had believed that Carson really did care for her. Now in the light of day, she'd begun to question that conclusion. After all, she'd never been a good judge of that sort of thing. And though he was clearly fond of her, he'd also made it clear he had no tolerance for liars.

Libby took another sip of ginger ale and sighed. It would be a relief to have the truth out in the open. Hopefully she'd have the chance to tell the whole story so that he would understand that she hadn't set out to deliberately deceive him. Libby paused and shrugged, deciding she'd have to skirt that issue. The deception had been deliberate. It was the falling in love with him had been purely accidental.

What if he loves me, too?

Her breath caught in her throat. He'd been so sweet and considerate last night. There had been genuine affection in his gaze. Strong emotions behind his kisses. But was that emotion love? Or only lust?

The thought niggled at Libby and a chill traveled up her spine. Stephen had been capable of being sweet and thoughtful, too. He'd even said he loved her. But, in the end, all he'd wanted was a physical relationship with her. Maybe that's all Carson wanted, too.

Odds were when she saw him tonight he'd ask again. The only question now was would he continue to come around when she said no?

"Are you sure you don't want to sit down and rest?" Carson slowed his footsteps to a stop, watching Libby closely. He cast a pointed glance at a bench just off the path. With the temperature hovering around seventy and only a slight breeze, the night had been perfect for a walk. But she'd been ill and they'd been walking for almost an hour.

"Will you quit worrying?" Libby slipped her arm through his and gave it a squeeze. "I feel wonderful. I think this fresh air is just what I needed."

Carson smiled and let his gaze linger. He had to

admit she looked a hundred percent better than she had last night. But he'd still been surprised when he'd picked her up and she'd suggested a walk along the beachfront.

Forgoing the bench, they continued down the long expanse of sand, holding hands. Though Carson was usually comfortable with silence, he made a conscious effort to keep the conversation going. Because any time there was a lull in the conversation, Libby got this look on her face that told him she was on the verge of quitting her job.

One of the wait staff had asked him earlier today when Libby's last day would be. Apparently Libby had mentioned her intent to leave at the end of the summer. It wasn't as if he didn't understand. School would be starting soon and he knew she was carrying a full load. Not to mention the bookings for her mother's catering business had soared since the successful event at Mrs. St. James's house.

Carson didn't know why he was trying to forestall the inevitable. After all, if she didn't tell him tonight, she'd just do it the next time they were together. He heaved a heavy sigh. He didn't want to see her quit. With him working so many hours, if their paths didn't cross at work, they'd barely see each other. And he didn't want that. Not when they'd grown so close.

His hope was that if she hung in there until the semester started, she'd be able to see that the job would fit in with her schedule. With Erin back from France, the demands of managing the food donations would be lessened and he'd be as flexible as he could with the office work.

Libby stopped suddenly and his heart sank. But when he turned his head he could see she had something more on her mind than work. She stared silently up at the sky.

He put his arm around her shoulder and she leaned back against him.

"This reminds me of when I was a little girl," Libby said finally. "A friend and I were in my backyard picking out constellations and I remember she said the strangest thing."

"Let me guess. Did she ask you to make a wish?" Carson's tone was teasing.

"No, that's what I expected." Libby smiled. "Instead she turned to me and said, 'Doesn't that remind you of God's promise to Abraham?'" Libby gave a little laugh. "Weird, huh?"

"God's promise to Abraham?" Carson thought for a moment. "That your children shall number as many as the stars in the sky?"

"That's what she said when I asked her what she was talking about." Libby shifted her gaze back to the stars. "Her comment that night surprised me. But I've since learned that people don't always say what we expect them to say. They don't do what we expect them to do. And often they aren't even who we expect them to be.''

It was much too philosophical a topic for such a lovely evening, Carson thought. She looked so beautiful in the moonlight. Her hair, pulled back in an amber clip, gleamed like polished ebony. She smelled like spring flowers. And when he'd kissed her earlier, she'd tasted like peppermint.

He smiled, remembering how hard he had to work for that kiss. When he'd leaned close, she'd turned her face, saying that she didn't want him to get sick. But when he'd told her he liked to live dangerously, she'd smiled and without warning *she'd* kissed *him.*

Her lips had been so warm and sweet that he could have sat in the Jeep and kissed her all night. But he'd forced himself to take it slow. Last night he'd pushed too hard and too fast and he didn't want to make the same mistake this evening.

Carson trailed a finger along her jawline, liking the healthy glow of color in her cheeks. ''I'm glad you're feeling better.''

''So am I.'' Her smile flashed briefly then faded. ''Carson, there's something we need to talk about—''

''Shh.'' He reached up and closed her mouth with his fingers. ''We don't need to talk right now, do we?''

Her eyes met his. After a long moment, she shook her head. ''You're right. Why spoil the evening?''

Her soft, slender hand traveled up his arm to his

shoulder, then her fingers slipped through the hair at the nape of his neck and she drew his head down to hers. Lost in the need reflecting in her eyes, he complied, watching as her lashes fluttered closed before their mouths touched.

Though Carson told himself to take it slow, the moment his lips met hers, he couldn't get close enough, couldn't drink in enough of her. It had been this way since the first time he'd seen her. It was as if he'd been waiting for her his whole life.

He deepened the kiss, deepening it, shifting one hand to cup the back of her head, holding her still. He wanted to loosen the clip that held her hair so that he could bury his fingers in the silky strands. He wanted her. Libby Summers. Now and tomorrow. For always.

He realized suddenly that he couldn't imagine not having her in his life. He'd been wrong to push her. He didn't want a summer romance or a quick fling, he wanted her.

By his side.

Forever.

Slowly, reluctantly, he drew back from her. Breathing shakily, he waited until she opened her eyes, feeling a wave of pure, male satisfaction at the dazed look in their depths.

"Marry me, Libby," he said, the unexpected words tumbling from his mouth in a rush of raw emotion. "I love you so much."

Chapter Twenty-One

Libby's heart stopped. "What did you say?"

Carson smiled then, his hand rising to cup her face. "Marry me."

"I don't understand." Confusion mingled with joy and spilled into her voice. She cleared her throat and struggled to pull her thoughts together.

But it was hard to think when he stood in front of her, his blond hair looking like a golden halo, his blue eyes shining with an intensity that both frightened and excited her.

"C'mon, Libby Summers," he teased, fingering a lock of hair that had pulled loose from the clip. "Is it that hard to make a decision?"

Summers.

Libby's blood ran cold. "Carson. There's something I need—"

"Carson, what are you doing out here?"

The feminine voice that sounded behind Libby was vaguely familiar. Libby groaned. Of all the times to be interrupted.

She turned and Carson's arm slid possessively around her waist.

"Audra," he said, the hint of tension in his voice telling Libby she wasn't the only one who resented Audra's untimely appearance. "Haven't seen you around lately."

"I've been spending more time in L.A." The blonde shrugged. "There's not much going on here."

"I don't know." Carson smiled affably. "Libby and I seem to keep busy."

"Libby?" Audra's dark-haired companion, who'd been standing back in the shadows, took a step forward. Recognition filled his eyes. "I thought that was you."

Libby's unease skyrocketed as she realized she knew the man. He'd been in her class at Princeton. They'd even gone out once or twice.

"Adam." She finally spit out the name. "What a surprise."

Carson's gaze slid from Libby to Adam then back to Libby again. "You two know each other?"

Libby wanted to grab Carson's hand and pull him down the sidewalk, far away from Audra. Far away from Adam. Far away from the words that would spill from his mouth and seal her fate. But her feet felt rooted in concrete and she couldn't move a muscle.

"Libby and I went to Princeton together." Adam warmed to the topic. "We were in the same study group. Way back when, we even dated for a while."

Libby smiled weakly and kept silent.

"I didn't know you went to Princeton," Audra said, her gaze narrowing. "You must not have graduated...."

"Not graduated?" Adam laughed out loud. "Where'd you get that idea? Libby graduated summa cum laude."

"What was I supposed to think?" Irritation crossed Audra's face at the patronizing tone in his voice. "She works as a waitress. You'd think if she'd graduated from Princeton she'd be doing something more with her life."

"A waitress? That doesn't sound like the Libby Carlyle I knew." Adam grinned and shook his head. "If I remember correctly, you had trouble carrying your own cup of Chai to the table without spilling it."

"Still does," Carson said. Suspicion colored his tone and his intent gaze fixed on Libby's face.

Libby merely smiled and shifted her gaze to Adam.

"I thought someone told me you'd started your own business," Adam continued as if he had all the time in the world to gab, and Libby suddenly remembered how much he liked to hear himself talk. "A boutique? An antique store?"

He wasn't going to give up, Libby realized. The muscles in her neck tightened into hard knots. "Antique store."

"That's what I thought." Adam smiled with satisfaction. "Do you still live in that house?"

It took every ounce of strength Libby possessed to stifle a groan. *Dear God, could this get any worse?*

"The one on Arrellaga?" Carson's ominous tone sent a shiver up Libby's spine.

"I don't know the address," Adam said. "All I remember is that we used to tease Libby about this old house she owned. I saw a picture of it once, and if I remember correctly, it was pretty cool."

The silence that followed was thick enough to taste and Libby waited for Carson to speak, waited for his anger to spill out. He had a right to be upset, she thought, nearly choking on her guilt. She'd lied to him. Told him she was someone she wasn't, claimed a past that wasn't hers. There was no good excuse she could offer, no real explanation. She could hardly explain that she'd wanted to find out if someone could like her for herself, without it sounding like some crazy game.

"Adam, honey." Audra placed one hand on his arm. "We'd better get going."

Libby breathed a sigh of relief. Unfortunately their departure was a few minutes too late.

"I'll give you a call next time I'm in town." Adam cast a questioning glance at Libby. "Are you in the book?"

Libby nodded, not daring to look in Carson's direction. She waited until Audra and Adam were out of sight before she turned to him.

He stood rigid at her side. Libby waited, hardly breathing, willing him to give her a chance to talk this out even though she had no idea what she would say to him.

"Libby Carlyle," he said finally, his voice stiff and stilted.

She lifted her chin. "That's my name."

"And Sierra Summers?"

"Sierra is my friend," Libby said. "She and I changed places for the summer. It was an experiment, one of those see-how-the-other-half-lives kind of thing," she finished weakly as his expression darkened.

"So it was all pretend." Carson's lips barely moved. His voice was flat, without the smallest trace of emotion.

"Not all of it." Libby touched his arm. "Not what I felt for you—"

"Stop it." He jerked his arm away. "No more lies."

"That's right." Libby grasped at his words like a drowning woman struggling to reach a life raft floating just out of reach. "No more lies. We'll get this all straightened out. You'll see. It's really not as bad as it seems.''

She was babbling and she knew it, but she couldn't stop. She had to keep him there so he could listen to her explanation, so he could understand that it was a harmless prank. Keep him there until he realized that nothing had changed. He was the same person. And she was the same person, too, just a few million dollars richer.

''It's over, Libby.''

Libby's heart convulsed but she wasn't about to give up so easily. ''We haven't talked. You haven't let me explain.''

''Explain what?'' Carson asked. ''That the person I fell in love with doesn't exist?''

His anger came through loud and clear, but it was the undercurrent of pain in his voice that tore at her heartstrings.

''I do exist,'' Libby said, softly touching his arm.

He shot her a steely glance and her hand fell to her side.

A knot formed in her stomach and though he still stood within arm's reach, Libby realized he was slipping away. ''Carson, please.''

''Please what, Libby?'' His gaze narrowed. ''Please tell you that it's okay? Please tell you I don't mind? Well, it's not okay and I do mind.''

''Carson—''

She opened her mouth to argue and he cut her off

with a sharp gesture of his hand. "No. No more lies. It's over, Libby. Over."

Libby stood in stunned silence. Why she was so surprised, she couldn't say. After all, hadn't she always known it would end this way?

Men always left her.

The only thing was that this time she couldn't blame the money.

She could only blame herself.

"I'm surprised you took the day off." Becca stared at Carson, a watchful look in her eyes. "What with it being Labor Day weekend and all."

Carson gave Seth a push in the playground swing and shot her a quick smile before turning his attention back to the boy. "Getting sick of me already?"

Although he was only teasing, Carson wondered if it could be true. After all, they'd spent more time together in the past two weeks than they had in the last six months. They'd gone to a concert in the park, a couple of movies and, of course, church.

Instead of attending services in Santa Barbara, Carson had gotten up early and driven to San Rafael. If he and Becca and Seth were going to be a family, attending Sunday services together was a good start. In fact he'd looked forward to it. It should have felt so right, sitting in the pew with Seth on his lap, Becca next to him and the morning sun streaming in through stained glass. But the experience had left Carson feeling strangely unsettled, like he was playing a role that didn't quite fit him. The role of his brother.

He shoved the melodramatic thought aside.

"I could never be sick of you." Becca tentatively touched his arm with her hand.

Carson turned to find Becca's gaze fixed on him. The look in her eyes coupled with the hint of pink coloring her cheeks told him she had something on her mind.

She wants me to kiss her.

That thought had flashed through his mind more than once recently. In fact, last night after they'd returned from the movie, she'd lingered by the door for the longest time. But all she'd gotten was a brotherly kiss on the cheek.

It was crazy but he felt to do more would be unfair to Becca. He still wasn't over Libby. Every time he saw a woman with dark hair and a slender build, he had to stop whatever he was doing and take a second look. He didn't know what he'd do if he actually saw her. Say hello? Shake her hand? Kiss her on the cheek?

His lips tingled remembering the feel of her skin beneath his mouth. He'd loved her with a passion that belied his pragmatic nature. It just showed how far astray he'd gone. Her lying had reinforced what he should have known all along—he was better to stay the course and focus on his responsibilities, beginning with Becca and Seth.

Carson returned his attention to the woman beside him, to the woman who would one day be his wife. A recent trip to a trendy salon in Santa Barbara had wrought magic. The blunt razor cut barely brushed her shoulders and flattered her heart-shaped face. Even her normally nondescript blue eyes looked larger and more luminous. Becca was attractive, he realized with surprise. "You look really nice today."

Becca's face brightened with pleasure and he realized he'd been too skimpy with the compliments.

"I like those shorts, too," he added.

Earlier in the week she'd gone shopping with his mother and had returned with several bags full of new clothes. The olive-green shorts she wore today showed off her shapely legs to full advantage while the white cotton shirt accentuated her tan.

"It's the haircut," she said, striking a vampish pose against the swing set post. "The stylist said it makes me look older, more mysterious."

Carson started, then chuckled when he saw the teasing light in her eyes. With brown hair, blue eyes and a sprinkle of freckles, Becca was more all-American, girl-next-door cute rather than mysterious.

"Yeah." Impulsively he leaned forward and fingered a lock of her hair. "Real mysterious."

"Carson?" Becca took a tentative step forward, placed her hands on his shoulders and lifted her face.

The questioning, almost pleading, look in her eyes was the only thing that stopped him from backing out of her arms. He reminded himself that this was what they both wanted and lifted a hand to caress her cheek.

"Mamma, push," Seth demanded as the swing slowed.

"In a minute, son," Becca said softly, keeping her gaze focused on Carson, her eyes wide.

Carson swallowed hard, feeling like an inexperienced fifteen-year-old on the verge of his very first kiss. But he wasn't a boy. He was a grown man and Becca would hardly be the first woman he'd kissed.

The image of Libby's mouth, all warm and soft flashed before him. An ache that had nothing to do with physical need and everything to do with a breaking heart washed over him. He'd missed Libby's kisses, but most of all he'd missed *her*—her irreverent attitude, her easy laughter, her zest for life.

Why had she lied?

The question had dogged him for days, but what did it matter anyway? She'd lied to him about who she was, about her family, about everything important.

"I never lied about what I felt for you...."

He shoved the memory aside and, with a resolute determination to leave the past behind, Carson lowered his head and brushed Becca's lips with his own.

When he started to pull back, she locked her fingers around his neck. "While that was nice," she said in a low voice, "something tells me you can do better. Kiss me like you really mean it."

But before he even had a chance to do as she asked, she crushed her soft lips to his.

The touch of her mouth stunned Carson, but after a second passed, and then another while her lips moved gently over his, Carson tried to abandon all rational thought and give himself over to sensation.

But still it was not enough. She was not Libby, he realized with the unsettling confusion of one waking from a dream. *Not Libby.*

Carson jerked back, pulling himself from her arms. He turned from Becca, his heart pounding in his chest, regret sluicing through his veins.

"Mamma, push," Seth called out, more forcefully this time.

Carson gave Seth's swing a big push, using the time to regain his composure before facing Becca. "That got out of hand. I'm sorry."

"I'm not." Becca lifted her chin. "I liked it."

"Becca." Carson struggled to find the words that would be not only honest, but kind. "I have to tell you I have trouble thinking of you in those terms. In so many ways you're like a sister to me."

"You didn't kiss me like a brother," Becca said matter-of-factly. "You enjoyed it as much as I did. We've had a lot of fun these past couple of weeks. You just need to give me a chance to show you how happy we can be together."

"It's not fair to you," he insisted.

"You let me be the judge of that." She shot him a wink. "I think you'll find I'm easy to love."

He had to laugh. And as he took her in his arms and gave her a hug, he could only hope her words were true and that one day he would love her half as much as he'd loved Libby.

Chapter Twenty-Two

Libby sat in the church pew wondering what had ever possessed her to agree to come to a music concert on a Tuesday night. She tried to think of a valid reason to leave early. One that Sierra and Peggy wouldn't immediately see through.

"This is fun." Maddie bounced up and down, her excited gaze shifting between the people in the audience and the band assembled in front of the church. "After the show, you and me and Mommy and Gram are all going out for ice cream."

"That sounds good." Even though it seemed that Libby's hopes for an early end to the evening weren't to be, she couldn't help but smile at Maddie's enthusiasm.

The little girl found pleasure in the smallest things...the hot-pink nail polish Libby had used on her nails, a friend from preschool waving broadly at her from across the church, the promise of an ice cream cone at the end of the evening.

Libby's gaze settled on Maddie's blond curls, remembering how, for one brief moment in time, she'd allowed herself to imagine having a little girl of her own one day.

Her heart twisted. She wondered if Carson ever ached for what might have been. If he ever wondered how she was or what she was doing. If he ever wished he'd given her a second chance.

She hadn't been able to stop thinking of him. It was ridiculous, she knew. But she couldn't help herself. She missed him so much. Missed his gentle teasing. Missed the way his dimple flashed in his left cheek. Missed the feeling of love and security she'd felt in his arms.

The band started their first set and everyone rose to their feet, clapping and cheering. Libby stood, finding the excitement of the crowd contagious. And as she joined in the singing of a popular song's refrain, she decided she was glad she'd come.

The past few days had been dreadful. Her mother had agreed to come for Thanksgiving but hadn't seemed at all enthusiastic. To top it off, Labor Day had come and gone with no sign of Carson. Not that Libby had really expected him to call, but she'd still foolishly hoped.

It was at times like this that Libby really wished

she could gain comfort from her faith. But nothing had changed. Despite Carson's inspiring story, she hadn't had a "mountaintop" experience.

The band slowed the tempo and Libby sank back in the pew, emotionally exhausted, content to let the music drift over her.

"That's a Steven Curtis Chapman song," Sierra whispered to Libby as the first chords of the next song sounded. "He's one of my favorites."

The song was compelling and Libby soon found herself immersed in the melody and in total agreement with the lyrics. There *was* more to life than living and dying, more than just trying to make it through the day. Despite all the advantages she'd been given, Libby realized that so far she hadn't done one thing to make the world a better place.

She pondered the thought as the next song started. This time it was the words about holding God's hand that struck a chord deep within her. Had she ever really put her life in God's hands? Had she ever really let God be a part of her life? Had she ever really let Him love her? Or had she treated God much the way she'd treated Carson, letting Him only get so close because she was afraid, fearful He'd see she wasn't good enough to love.

She pulled her hands together in her lap.

Dear God, it's me, Libby. I really want to turn my life over to You. But I'm afraid. I need Your strength and Your help. I'm willing to put my hand in Yours.

Just promise me You'll hold on tight like the song says. And that You'll always love me. Amen.

A sudden sense of calm settled over Libby as the warm, loving arms of her Heavenly Father closed around her. Libby sat very still, reveling in a sensation of total love and acceptance. Tears filled her eyes. After all this time of searching, she finally knew what unconditional love felt like.

"Aunt Libby?" Maddie whispered urgently, tugging at her arm. "I got a question."

Libby blinked back the tears and shifted her gaze to the little girl. "What is it, honey?"

"Can God really take us for a ride on an eagle?" Innocence filled the little girl's eyes.

At first Libby didn't understand what had prompted the strange question. Then she listened to the song the band was playing.

Libby smiled and tousled the little girl's hair. "God can do anything Maddie, even lift us up on eagles' wings."

Brian took a last sip of coffee and motioned to the waitress for the check. "I hear your friend Libby has been keeping herself busy."

"Is that so?" Carson's hand stilled on his wallet. During breakfast he and Brian had talked about everything…except the women in their lives. It seemed odd he'd bring up the subject now.

It had been six weeks since Carson had seen

Libby. She still haunted his dreams and he couldn't control that. But during the day he forced her from his mind every time a memory surfaced.

"She's opened a soup kitchen." Brian laughed as if he found the thought amusing. "Can you imagine luscious Libby serving soup to some down-and-outer?"

"I didn't think she was into such things," Carson murmured almost to himself.

"She's just another wealthy heiress with too much time on her hands." Brain's mouth turned up in a sardonic smile. "'Course, I suppose it beats maxing out the credit card or dallying with the pool boy."

Bitterness colored Brian's tone, telling Carson that Audra's betrayal had cut his friend deep.

"Speaking of former girlfriends," Carson said in as casual a voice as he could muster, "have you seen Audra lately?"

Brian shot Carson a narrowed glinting glance. "No, and that's just fine with me."

"She was such a good friend of yours."

"*Was* being the operative word," Brian said pointedly.

"Maybe there was a good reason she lied." For a second Carson wasn't sure if he'd spoken aloud or had just voiced the thought that had been running through his head since the night he'd found out Libby had betrayed *him*.

"There's no reason good enough," Brian said

flatly, handing the waitress his credit card and waving aside the bills Carson held out in his hand. "So, tell me, are you still dating your sister-in-law?"

"Becca was never married to my brother." Carson said the words slowly and distinctly so there could be no misunderstanding and no need to revisit this topic.

Brian lifted a brow. "Don't tell me you're in love with her?"

Carson wished he could say yes. He'd tried, oh how, he'd tried. Becca was a wonderful woman. But falling in love with her hadn't been as easy as he'd thought. "I care deeply for Becca. And you need to know that she and I have been talking marriage."

Brian gave a disgusted snort, pushed back his chair back and stood. "Face it, the only thing that woman has going for her is that she's got your brother's kid. Otherwise, you wouldn't give her a second glance. With all the women out there, hooking up with her makes no sense."

"Well, it does to me," Carson said, jutting his jaw out. "And that's all that matters."

"Are you sure you don't mind if we stop at the Farmer's Market on the way home?" Becca asked, stealing a quick glance into the back seat to check on her sleeping son.

"Not as long as we still have time to stop at a jeweler's," Carson said in a casual tone, slanting

Becca a sideways glance. "I thought we might look at a few rings."

"Rings?" Becca's breath caught in her throat. "As in an *engagement* ring?"

Carson shrugged. "I think it's about time, don't you?"

Though his lack of enthusiasm was a bit disconcerting, Becca hid her disappointment behind a bright smile. Up to this point they'd talked about marriage in only the most general of terms. And he'd never really popped the question, though she'd sensed he was getting close once or twice. Now it appeared he was skipping that step and moving on to the next.

She and Carson. Engaged.

Becca blew out a shaky breath, surprised she felt more scared than excited. After all, this was what she'd been hoping for since she'd given up hope of Cole coming back alive.

Unease traveled up her spine but she ignored it. She liked Carson. They had fun together. He would make her a good husband and he would be a wonderful father to her son. And despite what that nagging inner voice said, the fact that he looked like Cole didn't have a thing to do with her feelings for him.

They found a parking space a half block off State Street. They walked down the center of the downtown business district picking up an assortment of organically grown fruit and vegetables from various vendors. The last stop was for flowers to decorate the dinner table. It would be a celebratory dinner, Carson told Becca.

It was nearly time for the vendors to close up and the crowds were thick. Becca opted to wait on the sidewalk with Seth while Carson stood in line to pay for the flowers.

She told Seth to wave to Carson and his chubby hand opened and closed. Carson smiled and waved back just as a dark-haired woman who'd been crouched down picking through a bucketful of Gerber daisies rose suddenly and turned right into him, her hands full of flowers.

Carson automatically reached out to steady her. From where Becca stood, she couldn't see the woman's expression, but the stunned surprise on Carson's face took her breath away.

''Libby.'' Carson exhaled the word, his hands remaining on her arms long after her unsteadiness had passed.

Libby felt as if she'd been punched in the gut. She took a step back, forcing Carson to release his hold on her.

Though she'd known it was inevitable that their paths would someday cross, she'd pictured the chance encounter occurring at a social function or party. She'd thought she'd be wearing her finest evening wear, not blue jeans, a faded Princeton T-shirt and a ponytail sticking out from beneath a ball cap.

"They're for the soup kitchen." Libby thrust the daisies out for his inspection. The minute the words left her mouth, she wished she could call them back. Not only did the words fall far short of the easy self-assurance she wanted to project, Carson wouldn't have a clue what she was talking about.

To her surprise he nodded. "Brian told me you'd started a soup kitchen. There's been a real need in this community for some time. Good for you."

Libby waved aside the praise. It was the people of the various churches that volunteered, the restaurants that donated food, as well as the corporations that gave with their checkbook who deserved the credit. She was just the instigator, the coordinator, the glue that held it all together.

"I've wondered how you've been." His gaze lingered on her face.

Either he'd forgotten what she looked like or she still had that smudge of dirt on her cheek. Resisting the urge to pull out her mirror and check, Libby smiled instead. "You cross my mind every now and then, too."

The tension in his shoulders visibly eased. He returned her smile. "I know it's crazy, but every time I drive past Sunrise I think of you. Are you still into scones?"

Libby shook her head. "Scones have been replaced by chocolate-chip muffins. The problem is I can't find ones I like anywhere in town. Thankfully I got this fabulous recipe from one of my friends who loves to cook. Eventually I'll be back to the scones, but for now Peggy bakes up a batch every week or so...."

Libby stopped herself, realizing too late that she was nervously chattering about nothing.

"Peggy." His smile faded.

"That's right." Libby's smile never wavered. "She's my good friend. And a second mother to me."

His gaze searched her for a long moment and instead of the anger that had once filled the liquid-blue depths, all Libby could see was pain.

"I never meant to—" Libby had barely started speaking when the man behind Carson muttered under his breath and shoved past them, handing his money to the vendor. Only then did Libby realize that she and Carson were holding up the line.

She smiled an apology and quickly paid for her flowers before turning back to Carson. "If you want to talk, I have a few minutes. We could grab a quick cup—"

Carson shook his head. "I can't."

He glanced in the direction of the sidewalk and she followed his gaze. An attractive woman in her early twenties stood holding a sack of produce in one hand and the hand of a little towheaded boy in the other.

During the long days after they'd split, Libby hadn't believed her pain could be any worse. She'd been wrong. "I'd better go."

She walked away, praying he would call her back, but Carson remained silent and Libby kept walking.

"Mister, do you want those flowers or not?"

In a daze, Carson handed the man his money. Libby seemed different somehow, more open, more willing to talk.

Or maybe he'd been more open to listening…

"Who was she?" Becca's voice sounded from his side.

"Who was who?" he said absently, handing Becca the flowers and taking the heavy sack of fruits and vegetables from her.

"The woman," Becca persisted. "The one you were talking to."

Carson stared into the crowd as if he could still see Libby. "She used to work at the Waterfront."

"She's very pretty."

"Yes, she is."

Becca flashed a bright smile. "Are you ready to look at some rings?"

"Why don't we save that for another night?" Carson made a great show of looking at his watch. "It's getting late."

Chapter Twenty-Three

Carson sat next to Becca on the porch swing and placed an arm around her shoulder. Though he'd wanted to head straight home after dinner, retiring to the porch after helping his mother clean up the dinner dishes had become part of Becca's and his evening ritual and he didn't want to disappoint her.

Most evenings that he was in San Rafael, they would talk about their day and sometimes they would kiss. But the kissing had never again approached the intensity of that day on the playground. Since that incident Carson had never again let himself forget who he was kissing. It simply wasn't fair to Becca.

"Carson." Becca leaned her head back against his arm. "Have you ever done anything you've regretted?"

"I think we all have," Carson said softly, picking

up on the raw emotion in her voice. He let his hand fall to her shoulder in a comforting gesture.

"Lately I've found myself thinking a lot about Cole." A heavy weariness sounded in her voice. "Especially those last few weeks before he left for Africa."

"Becca, there's no need to talk about that—"

"There *is* a need," Becca interrupted. "If I don't talk about it, I'm going to go crazy."

"I know you two fought a lot before he left," Carson said slowly. "I'm not sure what about."

"Cole had been thinking about going on that trip for a long time," she said. "But I never thought he'd go through with it. He said I was selfish and didn't care about my fellow man."

"I take it you didn't see it that way?"

"I wanted him with me," she said simply, staring out into the darkness. "And if he wanted to serve mankind he could do it right here in California."

"He didn't want to do that?" Carson said, more as a question than a statement. He'd never understood his brother's desire to go to Africa.

"As far as I know he never seriously considered that option," she said. "But he may have. Toward the end I was too busy hurling accusations to listen."

Carson barely heard her words. After almost three years it was still hard for him to talk about his brother. "Why are you telling me this?"

"You and that woman today," Becca said slowly. "She was the one you'd been dating."

Carson shifted in the swing. "That's in the past—"

"Something happened between the two of you," Becca continued as if he'd not spoken.

"She lied to me," Carson said, surprised the admission made it past his lips.

"Why?"

"Does it matter?" He tried to keep the irritation from his voice. If he hated talking about Cole, he hated talking about Libby even more.

"Of course it matters." Becca turned in her seat to face him. "I suspected I was pregnant before Cole ever left for Africa, but his sanctimonious attitude made it impossible for me to tell him about the baby."

"You should have just sat him down and made him listen." Carson fixed his gaze on her.

"I tried," Becca said with a sigh. "But before I could get the words out, we started fighting about all the old issues. Then my pride stepped in. I wasn't about to beg anyone to stay with me. And I certainly wasn't going to dangle a baby that I didn't know for sure even existed in front of him."

"You think that's what I did to Libby," Carson said slowly. The realization hit him like a sledgehammer. "You think I made it so she couldn't tell me the truth."

"I don't know the situation well enough to say that." Becca shrugged. "But she had to know how much you valued honesty. It would certainly make it hard for her to admit she'd lied."

"She offered to explain." Carson's heart clenched as he remembered the desperation in her face. "But only after I'd learned the truth. Only when she didn't have a choice."

"Of course she had a choice," Becca chided. "Even then she could have refused to tell you anything."

It was a wonder she'd been willing to talk with him at all. He remembered with shame how he'd reacted and knew that his brother wasn't the only one prone to sanctimonious attitudes. "I refused to listen. I couldn't see how she could ever explain away her lies."

His matter-of-fact tone didn't fool Becca. Her eyes met his. "You miss her."

"I'm happy with you."

"You miss her," Becca repeated.

Every minute of every day.

"Sometimes," he admitted.

"You have the chance to undo the mistakes of the past," Becca said. "I'd give anything to be in your shoes. You can ask her to explain. You can listen to her side of the story. And, maybe if you're lucky, the two of you can move forward together."

"What about you and me?" Carson asked. "What about Seth?"

A hint of sadness crossed Becca's face. "I realized today that there is no you and me. Not really. Remember that old song lyric about two hearts that beat as one?"

Carson frowned. They were in the middle of a serious discussion and she wanted to play "Name that Tune"?

"No," he said. "And what does that have to do with anything anyway?"

"Even though he's gone, my heart still beats with Cole's." Becca raised one fisted hand to her chest. "You're a fine man, the brother I never had, my son's uncle and a terrific friend. But you're not Cole. I've been fooling myself into thinking there could be something more between us."

"When did you have this revelation?" Carson asked quietly.

"When I saw you looking into that woman's eyes," Becca said. "I realized that you looked at her the same way Cole used to look me. I had that once. I'm not going to settle for less. And you shouldn't, either."

"But what about Seth needing a father?" Carson asked. "What about Jimmy Bellows?"

"Jimmy? I can't see him as anyone's father. Least of all Seth's." Becca laughed out loud. "Seth will be just fine. He's got you and Connor. And that's good enough for now.''

"What about you?"

"I've got my memories," Becca said, a half smile lifting her lips. "And for now that will be enough."

Libby had just finished putting the groceries away when she heard a car turn into the drive. Sierra and Peggy were at a mother-daughter function at the church so it couldn't be them.

Pushing aside the lace curtains, Libby peered out the window. She immediately recognized the red Jeep. Her fingers shook as the curtains fell back into place. Her heart picked up speed. She barely had time to check her appearance in the dining room's large oval mirror before the doorbell rang.

Libby took a deep breath, trying to still the beating of her heart and pulled open the door. "Carson. What a surprise."

They carefully assessed each other. The dim porch lights cast mysterious shadows across Carson's classically handsome face as he looked down at her. His eyes seemed to glitter. Smile, Libby silently begged him. But he didn't. He just stared. Libby's hope drained away in the thick silence.

The shrill ring of the phone broke the impasse. Libby glanced at it gratefully. "I need to get that."

She waved him inside, then hurried across the dining room to the parlor.

Carson let the screen door fall shut behind him, but instead of following Libby into the parlor, he stopped at the dining room and took a seat, giving her some privacy.

Libby grabbed the phone, feeling oddly breathless. "Hello."

"Libby, darling." Her mother's voice sounded remarkably bright and cheery. "How are you?"

Libby's finger's tightened around the receiver. Her mother never called just to talk.

"I didn't expect to hear from you again until closer to Thanksgiving." Libby tried to keep her voice casual. "You're still planning to come, I hope."

"I'm afraid there's been a change in plans." There wasn't the slightest hint of apology in her mother's tone. "A group of us are going to Spain."

"Spain?" Libby sank into a nearby chair, unable to stop the disappointment welling up inside her.

"My friend, Matrice, has a villa there. She's invited several of her closest friends for an extended stay. We'll be there through Thanksgiving."

"What about…?" Libby paused, unable to recall the name of her mother's current boyfriend.

"Jean-Claude is coming, too," Stella said. "He's very excited about doing something different. The man isn't much of a traditionalist."

"It's been over two years since you've been back," Libby said finally when she found her voice.

"I know, darling." Her mother's voice softened. "There will be other holidays, I promise."

"Of course," Libby said automatically. "Another holiday."

Libby hung up before she realized she'd clicked off without saying goodbye. Libby shrugged, sure her mother hadn't even noticed. She was probably as eager to get off the phone as Libby had been. Libby exhaled a ragged breath and wiped a hand across her face.

"Are you okay?" Carson slipped into the love seat next to her, his voice filled with concern.

"I'm fine." Libby let her hair drop forward. She sniffed and hurriedly brushed aside the tears with the back of her hand.

"Change in plans?" His voice was deceptively casual.

"My mother," Libby said keeping her tone matter-of-fact. "She's decided not to come for Thanksgiving. Apparently she got a better offer."

The look in his eyes told Libby her bright smile hadn't fooled him. "Does she do this often?"

"She's good about making plans and even better at canceling." Libby shrugged. "I've never been certain if it's Santa Barbara she hates, or me."

"I don't see how anyone could hate you."

"You do," Libby said, meeting his gaze head-on.

"I do not," Carson said. "Far from it."

Libby leaned back in the high-backed chair, incredibly weary of the drama in her life. "Why are you here, Carson? What do you want from me?"

"The truth." His blue eyes were dark and intense. "I want to understand why you lied to me."

"What does it matter?" Libby said with a sigh.

Instead of getting angry, he reached over and took her hand. "Please, Libby. Just tell me."

There was a hesitation in the quiet voice that said this was no easier on him than it was on her. So, instead of arguing or simply refusing, Libby took a deep breath and went all the way back to The Chocolate Factory when the switch had first been conceived. She ended with the late-night encounter with Adam and Audra.

"I wanted to tell you so many times," she concluded. "But the time never seemed right."

"I can't believe you thought it would be fun to be poor." Carson shook his head in disbelief.

"It made perfect sense at the time. And I have to admit I learned so much more about myself and about other people. More than I ever thought possible." Libby returned his slight smile. "Now you know it all."

"Not everything," he said. "You left one question unanswered."

Libby thought back. Every question he'd asked she'd answered as openly and honestly as she could. "What one is that?"

He rose and dropped down to one knee before her. "Will you marry me?"

Libby stared at him and her heart clenched. "Is this some kind of joke?"

"I love you," he said. "From the first moment I saw you in the restaurant, I knew you were something special."

"A likely story." Libby answered with an automatic comeback then fought to swallow past the sudden dryness in her throat. "What about your girlfriend?"

Carson didn't even pretend not to understand. "Becca is like a sister to me, nothing more."

"Are you sure?" Libby had been hurt too often in the past to trust so easily.

"Libby," he said in a gentle tone, "you're the only woman for me. The only woman I want. The only woman I love."

She wanted to fall into his arms, to tell him she loved him, too. But part of her wondered if he would leave her, too. Just like her mother and all the others. To buy time she crossed her arms and looked him straight in the eye. "You haven't called me in six weeks."

"I was confused," he said softly. "But I never stopped loving you. I just needed Becca to remind me that life is too short to let foolish pride stand between me and the one I love. And I do love you, Libby, so very much. I want you to be my wife."

Libby thought of the way he'd hurt her by walking away that night on the beach. And the way she'd hurt him with her lies. Sometimes the one you love disappointed you. Love was a risk, she concluded.

"Could you give me your answer?" Carson offered up an exaggerated groan and a quick grin, but there was concern in his eyes. "My leg is cramping up."

Staring down at Carson's beloved face, Libby decided she had no choice. She'd learned at the church concert when she'd opened her heart to God that some risks were worth taking.

Libby laughed, letting her cares evaporate. "Yes."

"Yes?"

"Yes, I love you, Carson," she said, suddenly very sure of her decision. She captured his face in her hands. "And yes, I will marry you."

Joy flashed across his face.

"My heart was always yours," he said, bringing her hand to his mouth and kissing her palm. "And it always will be."

"And mine is yours."

"Two hearts beating as one," he murmured, rising to his feet and pulling her up to stand beside him.

"Forever," she repeated.

"For always," he said, his lips closing over hers.

Epilogue

"It's nearly time." Cherise, the wedding planner, adjusted Libby's veil, her gaze openly admiring. "You look absolutely beautiful."

Libby stared at her reflection in the large oval mirror. She'd been at the church for a couple of hours now, readying herself for the walk down the aisle. It was hard to believe the day she'd been looking forward to for the past six months had finally arrived.

She fingered the sheer softness of her veil and her heart picked up speed, imagining Carson's reaction. "How's my fiancé holding up? Is he getting nervous?"

Cherise busied herself with the veil. "Last time I checked he hadn't arrived yet."

If the woman sensed the sudden panic that raced through Libby at the knowledge that there was less than an hour to go until the wedding and the groom was missing, she didn't let it show. She smiled and patted Libby's arm reassuringly. "Don't you worry. He'll be here."

"He's here. I just saw him."

Libby recognized the feminine voice immediately. She whirled, her lips widening in unmitigated joy. "Mother!"

Stella Carlye stood just inside the doorway to the dressing room, as beautiful as ever, attired in a silk sheath that coordinated perfectly with Libby's colors. "Hello, darling."

"I can't believe you're here. I thought you weren't going to make it? What happened to your plans to go to—?" Libby stopped midsentence and clamped her mouth shut, realizing she was being rude. Her mother had barely walked through the door and here she was bombarding her with questions.

"Could you give us a few minutes alone?" Though the question was directed to Cherise, Stella's gaze never left her daughter's face.

"Of course." Casting Libby a curious glance, the woman brushed past Stella, pulling the door shut behind her.

A curious silence descended between the two women. Libby didn't know what to say. She still remembered that horrible night when her mother had called and said she wasn't going to be able to come.

"You told me there was absolutely no way you could make it," Libby said. "What changed your mind?"

"Are you happy I'm here?" Trepidation and uncertainty flickered across Stella's normally self-assured features.

"Of course I'm glad," Libby said simply. "I love you. You're my mother. You're the only family I have. I prayed you'd come."

"That's what he said," her mother murmured, but before Libby could ask who "he" was and what he'd said, Stella continued. "You're a very lucky woman to be marrying someone who loves you so much."

"Yes, I am," Libby said. "I can't wait for you to meet him."

"I already have," Stella said casually. "He picked me up at the airport. We had quite a nice conversation."

"He picked you up?" Libby paused, confusion furrowing her brow. "But how did he know when you were flying in?"

"He was the one who handled all the arrangements." Pink dotted her mother's cheeks. "He told me to forget the shares in Microsoft. He insisted the best gift I could give would be my presence at your wedding."

Libby thought about the last conversation with her mother. When Stella had insisted there was no way she could change her plans but said she had a nice wedding gift for them, Libby had hung up the phone and into tears. Between sobs she'd told Carson that not only didn't she care about any stupid stocks, she didn't even care about her mother.

It was untrue and Carson knew that, but he didn't call her on it. He just held her in his arms, kissed her tears and told her to trust him, that it would all be okay.

"He loves me," Libby said as if it were a new revelation instead of something she'd known since he'd come to her, heart in hand, that long-ago day and proposed.

"That's an understatement." Stella laughed but her expression quickly grew serious. "He's not the only one. I know I may not always show it, but I do love you, Libby."

Tears stung the back of Libby's eyes and her heart overflowed with joy. When she'd awakened this morning, she didn't think she could be any happier. But Libby knew now that she'd been wrong.

The dance floor of the country club overflowed with friends and family dressed in their wedding finery. But Libby barely noticed. Ensconced in Carson's arms, her head resting against his broad chest, it was as if they were the only two people in the room...maybe in the world.

Libby snuggled up against him and sighed with happiness. Her best friend. Her husband.

"Sierra and Matt seem to be having a good time," Carson whispered against her hair. "Check it out."

Libby lifted her head and shifted her gaze to a table on the edge of the dance floor where a man and a woman sat, holding hands and talking. The handsome dark-haired man was looking at Sierra as if she were the only woman in the room.

"They're in love," Carson said.

Libby smiled and met his gaze. "Like you and me."

Carson lowered his head and captured her lips in a long lingering kiss, a kiss laced with promise and pent-up passion.

"Hey, you two." Brian's teasing voice broke through the romantic haze. "You'd better save some of that for later."

Libby could have come up with a quick quip. After all, Brian thrived on such repartee. But at the moment Libby had more important things on her mind. By the time the kiss ended and Libby looked up, Brian and Audra were already halfway across the dance floor.

"I can't believe they're together," Libby said.

"For now," Carson said with a laugh. "Brian's track record for long-term relationships leaves something to be desired."

"I hope they make it," Libby said.

"You do?" Surprise sounded in Carson's voice.

"Of course," Libby said. "I want everyone to be as happy as we are."

Her gaze flickered over the family and friends who'd gathered for the wedding. She caught sight of her mother standing next to a colonnade, looking far too young to be any bride's mother. She was laughing with Carson's mother who held a sleepy Seth in her arms. Libby smiled at the little ring bearer. He'd done remarkably well, thanks to flower girl Maddie who'd firmly held his hand at the front of the church when he'd wanted to go searching for his mother.

Libby found Becca on the dance floor. Although Becca seemed to be having a good time, Libby knew how hard this wedding had been on her. A couple of weeks ago, the two women had sat down and Libby had heard all about Becca's ill-fated romance with Cole Davies.

To find the love of your life and then lose him...

Her fingers tightened around Carson's hand. "Promise me nothing will ever happen to you."

Carson followed the direction of her gaze and understanding filled his eyes.

"I'll always be there for you, Libby," he said softly. "And for our children."

As his lips closed over hers, Libby thanked God again for His precious gift. A gift more precious than gold or silver. And a gift she would treasure the rest of her life.

* * * * *

If you enjoyed TWO HEARTS,
you'll love Cynthia's next book,
LOVE ENOUGH FOR TWO,
coming in August 2004.
Don't miss it!

Dear Reader,

I'm often asked what's behind a book's story line. In coming up with the idea for *Two Hearts*, I reached way back into my childhood.

Do you remember the Mark Twain classic *The Prince and the Pauper?* Of course, Libby is a rich heiress rather than a prince, and the story takes place in modern-day Santa Barbara rather than sixteenth-century London, but just like the Prince of Wales, Libby learns so much by walking in another's shoes.

She also receives some additional blessings—the love of her life and a closer relationship with God. In the end, who could ask for anything more?

Wishing you your own happily-ever-after,

Cynthia Rutledge

Love Inspired®

LOVE IS PATIENT

BY

CAROLYNE AARSEN

There was more to Lisa Sterling than met the eye.
Dylan Matheson's new secretary was hiding
something—the reason why she was working for
him. Accompanying her boss to a family wedding
showed Lisa a softer side to the businessman. When
her secret was revealed, could God make Dylan see
that love was all things, including forgiveness?

Don't miss

LOVE IS PATIENT
On sale April 2004

Available at your favorite retail outlet.

Visit us at www.steeplehill.com

LILIP

Visit Steeple Hill Books online and...

EXPLORE new titles in Online Reads—new romances every month available only online!

LEARN more about the authors behind your favorite Steeple Hill and Love Inspired titles—read interviews and more on the Authors' page.

JOIN our lively discussion groups. Topics include prayer groups, recipes and writers' sessions. You can find them all on the Discussion page.

In today's turbulent world, quality inspirational fiction is especially welcome, and you can rely on Steeple Hill to deliver it in every book.

Steeple
Hill®

Love Inspired®

HERO IN HER HEART

BY

MARTA PERRY

Nolie Lang's farm, a haven for abandoned animals, gave hope to the disabled. Working with the injured firefighter Gabriel Flanaghan, who refused to depend on anyone, including God, tested her faith. Could Nolie make Gabe see that, no matter his injuries, he would always be a hero in her heart?

Don't miss

HERO IN HER HEART
On sale April 2004

Available at your favorite retail outlet.